"Emotional and brilliant…"

"Tastefully erotic … more smart than smutty…"

"Powerful and compelling…"

MY MATE JACK

A HEATED BEAT STORY

GARRETT LEIGH

FOREWORD

My Mate Jack is set in a time before smartphones and instant messaging. Be patient with these boys as they navigate their sexual discovery / awakening through dial-up internet.

MY MATE Jack was the first bloke I ever fancied. Not that I knew what it meant back then. At twelve years old, who did? Not me. All I knew was the brush of Jack's leg against mine was the catalyst for my first boner, and it was three long fucking years before it happened again….

CHAPTER ONE

1999

Towcester, England.

WILL WATCHED the empty Hooch bottle spin in the center of the circle. To his right sat Ginny, the fittest girl in year ten. All the boys in the circle had their eye on her, praying the spinning bottle would make their wet dreams a reality. They all wanted to snog Ginny. Every one of them except Will.

The bottle stopped. There was a collective whoop.

"Jackie-boy," Woody crowed. "'Bout bloody time."

Will's heart skipped a beat. If Ginny was supposed to be the fittest bird at school, Jack Lawson was definitely the fittest bloke. Tall, with floppy sandy-brown hair and dark eyes. Striker on the football team. Banging DJ. He even played the drums in a local band—sweating, biceps popping. Did it get any hotter than that?

Not if Will's dirty dreams were anything to go by.

Jack sat up and crawled to the center of the circle. He took the bottle and spun it again, chucking a wink Ginny's way before he sat back. Everyone knew she had the hots for him. It was the talk of the school. Not that Jack seemed to care. He didn't give a toss what anyone said about him. Never had.

The bottle slowed. It stuttered past a few faces. Nearly stopped. Kept going. Then it landed on….

Shit. It's pointing at me.

Will gulped and felt heat flood his cheeks. Jack was his next-door neighbor and best friend and the only soul in the world who knew his secret. One of them, at least.

He doesn't know how much I want to kiss him.

Jack crawled forward on his hands and knees, his grin evil. He stopped a foot away from Will, oblivious to the leering catcalls of their friends around them. "Pucker up, blondie."

Is he serious?

Will knew he wasn't. He couldn't be, but that didn't stop the thunder of his heart as Jack leaned ever closer.

Jack stopped with his face an inch from Will's. Licked his lips. Winked. Will felt like he might faint. The split-second pause felt like an hour. Then he lunged at Jack, shoved him across the grassy circle, found a grin from the pit of his stomach and plastered it on his face. "Piss off, you knobber."

There were loud boos around them. More catcalls and whoops. Woody jumped on Jack and pretended to hump him. Everyone laughed. Someone passed Will a spliff and he forced himself to join in.

He took a deep drag. Summer nights at the park were always like this: some bootlegged booze, a bit of weed, and always, *always*, spin the bottle, a game Will would lose whoever the bottle pointed at. The night wore on. He watched Jack kiss Ginny, Paige, and Meg and tried not to cringe. He wasn't jealous. Didn't have any right to be. But that didn't make it any easier. They'd been hanging around the cricket pavilion in the park their whole bloody lives and nothing ever changed.

Will loaded up on sugary alcopops and blazed a few more joints. Watching Jack snog birds didn't seem so bad through the haze of being stoned. Around eleven, the Friday night gathering began to break up. It wasn't a school night, but most kids had curfews. Will watched them go and tried not to scowl as Ginny smothered herself all over Jack, trying to needle him into walking her home.

"Aw, babe, you live miles away," Jack countered. "Rob's going your way. Walk with him."

Rob looked like the cat who'd got the cream. Ginny, not so much, but Jack got his way, as usual.

Jack always got his way.

Ginny left and before long Will and Jack were alone in the dark park, just the two of them, like it would be for the rest of the night. Jack always slept at Will's on Friday nights. Will's dad worked graveyard shifts as a warehouse manager, so Jack kept Will company all night long, from a distance, at least, curled up on the beat-up sofa bed in Will's bedroom.

Jack thumped Will's shoulder. "Come on, mate. Let's go back to yours and get some more beer."

They walked home, bypassing the boisterous high street and slinking down the alleys they knew so well, hands in pockets, hoods up. Jack was quiet for most of the way. Will glanced at him a few times, curious. Jack usually talked his ear off. Maybe he was drunk. Will was having trouble putting one foot in front of the other himself.

Didn't stop him helping himself to his dad's stash of Stella when they got home.

He cracked open the bottles and led the way upstairs to his room. Jack opened the window and pulled out his cigarettes. He could've smoked the whole way home, but it was part of their routine to crawl out onto the porch ledge and smoke a couple of fags before they both passed out.

Jack hoisted himself up on the windowsill and clambered out. Will joined him at the open window and accepted the proffered smoke. They lit up in silence and blew smoke to the stars. It was a while before Will felt Jack's gaze on him.

Will tapped ash into the plastic guttering. "What are you staring at?"

Jack shrugged. "I want to ask you something."

"So?" Will considered Jack. It wasn't like him to be shy. "Ask me, then."

"You've never snogged a bloke, have you?"

Will choked on his beer. Of all the things he'd expected Jack to say, that wasn't one of them. Will had told him he liked boys a few years ago, by accident more than anything else, his tongue loosened by the bottle of Bailey's they'd pinched from Jack's nan, but they hardly ever talked about it. It wasn't even an elephant in the room. It just… was.

Will gathered himself. "Why do you want to talk about me snogging?"

"Why not?" Jack lit another cigarette. "I saw the way you looked at me tonight."

Will felt suddenly sober as a bloody judge. Despite the cool night air, sweat trickled down his back. "You did?"

"Yeah." Jack blew a set of perfect smoke rings. "You were fucking petrified. How's that going to look when you finally meet the bloke of your dreams, eh? You need to get out there, mate."

Oh. Will's heart felt strange. Not good or bad… just strange.

"Maybe you should go out with a few girls." Jack made his suggestion like it was the most logical thing in the world.

Will felt sick. "What the hell for?"

"Practice," Jack said. "It's all the same, innit? Upstairs, at least."

Will laughed, though he died a little inside. He'd kissed his fair share of girls in the park after school. He'd had to… to save face. After the first time, he'd gone home and cried himself to sleep, but he'd got over that and built up a healthy collection of gay porn on his computer to ease the pain. "I'm not going to ask out any birds, Jack. Rather shoot meself."

"No need to get dramatic." Jack finished his smoke and scrambled inside. He sat on the edge of Will's bed and kicked off his shoes. "You can practice on me if you want."

"What?"

4

Jack shrugged like it was no big thing. "I'm not gay or anything, but I messed about with a dude in Majorca last year. Tossed him off, too. It was fun."

Will sat his beer bottle down. Scrutinized the label to check he hadn't picked up a bottle of paint thinner. He had to be dreaming, right? "You never told me that."

"Forgot about it. You were down the coast in Skeggy with your nan when I got back."

So? Will didn't voice his question. He picked the label off his beer bottle instead and tried to calm his racing heart. Jack with a bloke? What the actual fuck? "Weren't you going out with Clare last summer?"

Jack pulled a face. "She was shagging Craig Poulter the whole time I was away, remember?"

That rang a bell. Will had never liked Clare. She was pretty enough, if you like that kind of thing, but she had a name for being a bit of a slag. Jack deserved better than that. "Can't believe you got off with a guy. Was it weird?"

"Not really. Kissing him was cool, and the hand job was like having a wank, you know? Only we did it to each other."

"He tossed you off too?" Will didn't know what to say. How was Jack getting to do all this shit first? Will was supposed to be the gay one, dammit. And his mind was reeling. He wanted to know every little thing about Jack's holiday dalliance, and more than that, he wanted to get back to the bit about practicing snogging on each other, but he couldn't find the words. Perhaps he had misheard Jack after all.

"So, are you game, or what?"

Will blinked. "Eh?"

Jack laughed. He lay back on Will's bed and folded his arms behind his head, all dark eyes and shaggy hair. "You're such a dreamer. No wonder you don't notice any blokes. I was saying we could practice kissing if you want. You know, so you're not nervous next time the bottle lands on you."

This time Will couldn't stop the beer going down the wrong way. He coughed. "Next time? What are you going to do? Out me to the whole school by snogging my face off? I'd rather smooch the girls."

"Liar." But Jack looked sheepish all the same. "Okay, maybe we shouldn't mess around in front of other people, but I still reckon you should try your techniques out on me. Ginny says I'm the best kisser in the whole school, and she should know." Jack swooned and pitched into a fit of weed-fueled giggles.

Will dove at him and pushed him off the other side of the bed. "It's not funny, arsehole. I'm the only gay in the whole bloody town. I'm going to die a virgin at this rate."

Jack hit the floor with a thump. He lay there a moment, still laughing, then hauled himself back onto the bed. "Chill out, mate. No one said anything about bonking."

Will tried to grin. *Chill out.* Yeah, right. Jack had been taking the piss since that stupid bloody bottle had put the idea of them kissing in his daft head. "You're not funny."

Jack sobered and stared with an expression Will couldn't decipher. "I wasn't joking, at least not about the kissing part. We're friends, right? Ginny and Meg snog all the time."

He had a point. The girls were always messing around with each other, and Will had often watched them and maligned the fact that girls had it easy... from his point of view, at least. They could do whatever they wanted and no one cared. It would be a different story if Will jumped on Jack in the middle of the park. Snogged his face off and squeezed his arse.

So why not do it here? No one will ever know.

Will stared at Jack as his mind shouted, *What if? What if? What if?* He wanted to kiss Jack—fuck, yeah, he wanted to kiss Jack—but Jack had kissed loads of girls. What if Will was crap? Fuck. What if Jack laughed at him... or hated him after? Will fancied the arse off Jack, but beyond all that shit, Jack was his best friend. He couldn't—

"Fuck's sake," Jack growled, exasperated, and lunged across the bed. The shove came as little surprise—they'd spent their whole lives horsing around—but when Will found himself on his back, still on the bed instead of arse over tit on his bedroom floor, he knew something had changed.

Jack restrained Will, panting. "Stop freaking out," he said. "You're right about this closeted bloody town, so let me help you."

"Help me?" Will tried to sound indignant, but with Jack's body pressing into him in all the best—worst—no, best, definitely best, ways, it was… uh, hard.

Jack grinned and rolled off Will, granting him a much needed reprieve, but he didn't go far. He stretched out beside Will and propped his head on his hand. "Look, I know I'm pretty useless when it comes to all this gay stuff you're probably dealing with, but I can do this for you. I want to."

He wants to kiss me. Will knew the interpretation was dubious… generous and flawed, but the offer was tempting. Too tempting. Will shifted over, faced Jack, and looked him in the eye for the first time since the bizarre conversation had begun. "What… I mean, how…."

Jack tapped his finger to Will's lips. "Just relax. I know what I'm doing."

Will didn't doubt that, but as Jack leaned forward he found himself anything but relaxed. Jack touched his shoulder. Will jumped a bloody mile.

"Relax," Jack said again. "You know, all the girls fancy you. They reckon you've got a girlfriend at your nan's place or something, and that's why you won't go out with any of them."

"Why would they think that?" Will tried not to notice Jack had edged closer… close enough that Will could feel his warm, smoke-laced breath on his face.

Jack shrugged. "I might've dropped a few hints. I know you don't want to tell anyone yet."

How do you know that? You've never asked me. But Will's questions went unsaid, cut off by the brush of Jack's lips on his. Will froze, and the world as he knew it ceased to exist.

Jack kissed him over and over until Will finally let out the breath he'd sucked in the moment he'd felt Jack's soft lips on his.

Jack smiled, still half kissing Will. "That's it. Not so bad, eh?"

Bad? Fuck, no. Will took another breath and went looking for another go. Jack chuckled and parted his lips. Will deepened the kiss, almost by accident, and sucked Jack's bottom lip into his mouth. Tasted it. Ran his tongue all over it. Jack made a sound—a moan, a grunt—Will wasn't quite sure, but, *God*, he felt it. Felt it all over him, from his tingling scalp to his curling toes. Will's heart beat like a train. He pulled Jack closer, thrust his hands into his soft hair, and then they were kissing again… really kissing, like they'd never, ever stop. Will held Jack's chin in his hand and explored his mouth with his tongue, every bump and ridge. He kissed Jack with all he had until he realized they'd both forgotten to breathe.

Will pulled away, slowly, his eyes squeezed shut, like if he opened them Jack would evaporate and his first ever kiss would be another figment of his overactive imagination.

Jack laughed, breathless. "Wow. Don't think you've got much to worry about."

"Really?" Will cracked open an eye. "Was I okay?"

"Okay? You might be a bloke, but that's the best snog I've ever had."

Will blushed; he couldn't help it. He pressed his face into the pillow, glad they hadn't bothered to turn on the lights. "I haven't got much to compare it to, but it was pretty good for me too."

Jack snorted. "It was better than good, mate. Like it should be."

"Yeah." Will didn't know what else to say. His pulse had slowed to a steady gallop, but inside he still burned… his lips, his tongue. And he didn't dare look down. Couldn't face the swollen heat in his jeans.

Jack rolled onto his back. Will didn't have to look to know

he was staring at the ceiling. "Are you ever going to tell your dad?"

Will closed his eyes. It was a question he'd asked himself every day since the first time Jack's mere presence had set his world on fire, and he was still no closer to an answer. Will's dad was nothing like Jack's, who spent much of his time away on dubious business trips, chasing any skirt who wasn't his wife. Instead, widower Ned Barter was honest, hard faced and hard working. Loved Will and provided for him. Let him live his own life. Didn't care if Will and Jack smoked fags on the porch roof or pinched his beer. But telling him his only child… his only *son* was gay?

Will wasn't sure he'd ever be ready for that. "Maybe I'll tell him before we go to uni. Drop it on him, then fuck off somewhere really far, like Scotland or something."

Jack sniggered. "Sounds like a plan, for you at least, but I've told you a hundred times. I'm not going to uni."

"Yeah, yeah." Will had heard it all before. If Jack had his way, he'd be out of school… and Towcester… before the ink had dried on his last exam paper, but his parents, particularly his twat of a father, had other ideas. "You might change your mind if you get good A-levels."

"Nope. No chance." Jack sat up, though he didn't move away from Will. Didn't move the leg pressed against Will, warming him from the inside out. "Fuck that uni shit. I'm gonna get a residency in Ibiza. Spend the rest of my days in the sun."

Will rolled his eyes. "You and your bloody DJ crap. What are you going to do when you're old? Be Terry feckin' Wogan?"

Jack sighed, like he so often did when Will didn't understand him. "Drum-and-bass, Will. Not fucking radio."

Will knew that, really, but winding Jack up was too much fun, and it helped him pretend Jack wasn't so cool. That Will wasn't his geeky companion, the trusty sidekick no one ever noticed hanging around the hot guy mixing it up on the decks at local underground raves. The raves not even Will's dad knew they went to.

"Hey, Will?"

Will refocused on Jack. He hadn't noticed him rolling over again. "Yeah?"

"How was it for you? The kissing, I mean? I know you hated kissing all those girls. I wanted this… I didn't want it to be shit when you kissed a bloke too."

Jack chewed on his lip, and Will stared. They'd been friends for more than a decade, and he'd never seen Jack do that. The gesture was uncertain… nervous, and not the Jack Will knew at all.

Will touched Jack before he knew what he was doing. He gripped his shoulder, then slid his hand down his arm, found Jack's fingers, and twined them with his own. "Jack, it was amazing, but—"

"Yeah?" Jack's voice was barely a whisper, his lips just a hairbreadth away even as Will closed the distance between them.

"You said it was practice, right? So I could get better?" Jack nodded. Will smiled. "Then I think I need to do it again… and again, just to make sure."

CHAPTER TWO

2002

Towcester. England.

"Come on, mate. Plenty more fish in the sea and all that."

Will ignored Jack and stared morosely into his empty pint glass. "Easy for you to say."

Jack snorted. "Is it?"

Will glanced up. They were sitting in the garden of their local pub, nursing the beers they'd only just become old enough to buy and trying to drink off a heavy night of raving the night before. "Don't give me that shit. You're with a different bird every week. I was with Dave for six months."

"I know, I know." Jack slung his arm around Will in a fraternal, placating hug. He smelled of sweat and wood smoke and a long night mixing dirty beats under the stars. He smelled of Jack. "But look at it this way: at least you can go off to uni now without anyone tying you down. Live a little, mate. I know you really liked Dave, but it wasn't like you were love's young dream, was it?"

Jack had a point. Dave had been nice enough… good-looking in a boyish way and easygoing, the perfect guy to take home to his dad a long year after his big confession. But Will had known the whole time they were together that some-

11

thing was missing: that fire, that burn. Will had done every-thing he could think of with Dave, testing the waters, trying new things, but none of it compared to those simple kisses he'd shared with Jack so long ago. The kisses that would be seared on his soul forever.

Will wasn't about to tell Jack that, though. It had been three years since his first kiss had lasted all night long, and they never talked about it. And since that very first time, Jack had never mentioned his mysterious Majorcan encounter either.

Will sighed and tried to pull his mind back to Dave, the lost love he was supposed to be mourning. "I can't believe he dumped me over the phone. Said he thinks we should just be friends. That's so bloody lame."

Jack rubbed Will's shoulder. "I know, but it just proves the bloke was a goon. He only wanted you for your sexy body."

"Shut up." Will shoved Jack off him. He'd filled out over the past few years, put some muscle on his lean frame, but he was still a skinny streak of nothing compared to Jack.

"Your dad didn't like him."

"Eh? What makes you say that?"

Jack shrugged. "He told me. Said talking to Dave was like a Coldplay album. One good song, then the rest like listening to a sofa yawn."

Will glared. It sounded like the sort of gem his dad would say, but why the hell had he said it to Jack and not Will? Though, in truth, his dad had taken little notice of Will's growing confidence in his sexuality. Even Will's big coming out speech had been an anti-climax:

"Dad, I think I'm gay."

"All right, son. Do you still like footie?"

That had been that, and Jack and his father aside, Will didn't care what anyone thought. He hadn't bothered to come out at school; he'd just stopped denying the rumors about him and the second guy he'd ever kissed.

Jack drummed his fingers on the table, full of rhythm and

energy, even beneath the weight of two hours' sleep. "Can I ask you something?"

Will stubbed his smoke out in the overflowing ashtray. "This isn't about bum sex again, is it?"

Jack had the good grace to look sheepish. Once Will had come out and started meeting guys, Jack had been full of questions that often made Will squirm. "Kind of. You and Dave, did you ever, you know, actually do it? You never told me."

"You never asked." Will covered his flush with a swig of beer. Jack had asked lots of things, but never that, and come to think of it, he'd stopped asking questions when Will had started seeing Dave.

"Figured you didn't want to talk about it."

Will snorted. "So what's changed? Did my flashing gay boy V-plates fall off?"

"What? No. I was just wondering. That's all."

Will felt bad then. Jack was his biggest supporter, strong and loyal. Will wasn't naïve enough to believe being gay in their close-knit hometown would've been so painless without Jack by his side. Everyone in Towcester knew Jack would deck anyone who gave Will shit. "Okay, shoot. What do you want to know?"

"Um…." Jack drained his drink. "Hang on a sec."

Will watched Jack disappear into the pub, presumably to get more drinks. Then he slumped and put his head on his folded arms. Trailing Jack around the southeast while he DJ'd at squat parties and dodgy underground clubs was a blast, but it was fucking exhausting. Will loved the grimy beats of a proper stomping rave, loved watching Jack do what he loved most, but after a long weekend of partying, he needed his bed.

"So…." Jack put two more pints of lager on the table. "Tell me as much as you want to."

Will eyed the full glass, unsure what he wanted to do least: drink another pint or confess his boy-sex secrets to his oldest friend. "We did fuck, if that's what you really want to know."

"You did? When?"

Will thought back. "Just before Christmas. He stayed a couple of days while Dad was on nights and you were off shagging… what was her name again? Carly?"

"Charlie." Jack scowled, but he looked too curious to be truly annoyed. "So what happened? Did you, um…."

"Get fucked up the arse?"

Jack grimaced. "I wasn't going to say that."

"I know. You were going to stammer through a bunch of bullshit euphemisms first, so I saved you the trouble. And in answer to your question, yes, I did get fucked."

Jack took a long swallow of his drink. Will could tell he was bracing himself. "Did you like it?"

Will thought back to the night he'd decided he was finally ready to lose his virginity. It had been an awkward, messy encounter, but not one he regretted. "Not at first. It *really* hurt. I punched Dave in the chest and made him take it out."

"Nice. Bet that ruined the mood."

"Not really." Will shrugged. "Dave had done it before, so he knew what it felt like. He got me through it and it was good after that."

"Good?"

"Yeah, good."

Jack traced the rim of his glass with his fingertip. "Sex should be better than good, Will. Remember?"

"If you say so." Will let the sentence hang, hoping Jack would drop the subject. Talking about dirty stuff with Jack had never been awkward, but Jack looked uncomfortable, like he wished he'd never brought it up, and he didn't say anything for a while.

Will let himself drift. Jack looked lost in thought and that suited Will. Companionable silences had always been one of his favorite ways to kill time with Jack. He'd miss it when they parted ways in just a few weeks, Will to visit his nan and then study graphic design at uni in Leeds, and Jack to see out the rest of the summer in the job of his dreams in Ibiza. For the first time ever, they wouldn't be spending the summer holidays together, and it was the longest they'd been apart since they were six years old. Will was trying not to consider the very real possibility that Jack wouldn't come back, that he'd find the life and love he'd dreamed of and never come home.

Yeah. Will was going to miss more than the silence. He was going to miss Jack so much his stomach clenched whenever he thought of it. They were both seeing through plans they'd cooked up years ago—together—and everything was slowly falling into place, but *fuck* it hurt.

"Wakey wakey." Jack shook Will's shoulder. "Let's go home. I reckon I could sleep for a week."

Will roused himself, dopey from an afternoon on the beer. They'd come to the pub to stretch out the day so they wouldn't crash too early and wake up in the middle of the night. Their A-level exams were done, but they both had student jobs first thing Monday morning.

They walked home in another one of those easy silences. They bumped into each other from time to time, both exhausted and slightly drunk. When they reached their street, Jack turned toward his own house. Will caught his arm. "Do you want to come over for a bit? You can kip on the sofa bed."

"The sofa bed?" Jack feigned offense and Will grinned. It had been years since Jack had last slept on the sofa bed. After that first night of kissing, they'd fallen asleep in Will's bed, side by side, not touching, but feeling each other's warmth. Since then, Jack had always slept in Will's bed.

"Come on." Will turned toward his house. "Let's go home."

They were side by side in Will's bed before either of them spoke again, watching *Match of the Day 2* through hooded eyes. Will was half-asleep when he felt Jack roll over and face him.

"Will?"

"Hmm?" Silence. Will cracked an eye open to find Jack wide-awake and staring at him. "What's up?"

"Do you remember a few summers ago when I let you practice, uh, snogging on me?"

As if Will could forget. "Yeah. Why?"

"Do you think...?" Jack stopped and twisted Will's faded sheets into a tight, tense knot. "Do you think you could do that for me? I mean, not with just kissing, I mean... like, with, uh, going all the way...."

"Eh?" Will hauled himself upright. Jack looked like he wanted the bed to swallow him up. "What do you mean?"

Jack sighed. "I don't want to go to Ibiza a virgin, but I don't want to shag any of the mangy girls around here either. Don't want the whole town's sloppy seconds, you know?"

Will took a moment to process the news that Jack was still a virgin. He'd had a ton of girlfriends that year alone. Had he really not been shagging *any* of them? Then the gravity of what Jack was asking him hit him like a truck. "You mean... you want to... bloody hell, with me?"

Jack shrugged. "We're best mates, right? I trust you, you trust me. And we've snogged before. That didn't feel weird."

"But you're straight," Will blurted. "And kissing is different. Why would you want to have *sex* with me?"

"Why not? You're hot, Will. All the girls say so, and I know you won't laugh at me if I fuck it up. I mean, come on. How many eighteen-year-old virgins do you know? I can't go to Ibiza and not know what I'm doing."

"I'm not a bird, Jack. It won't be the same." *Won't be.* Will noted his own choice of words and realized he was actually considering Jack's request.

"I know that." Jack leaned forward, like he sensed Will wavering. "It's harder, innit? To get it in? So being with a bird after will be easier, won't it?"

A painful combination of a laugh and a cough escaped Will. "I guess."

"So… will you do it? Let me try with you?"

"Um, okay." Will's heart was in his throat. *I'm going to have sex with Jack*. Despite the weirdness, knowing Jack could have anyone he wanted made Will kind of touched he'd chosen him to be his first. "When do you want to do it?"

"Now?"

Okay, make that touched and totally fucking terrified. Will scrambled out of bed. "I need a shower. Think about it while I'm gone, yeah? I won't be offended if you change your mind."

He left Jack to do just that and fled to the bathroom. They'd both showered when they'd crawled home from the rave that morning, but Will was sweating already, and he couldn't bear the thought of the smell of man turning Jack off. Besides, if Jack was serious, there were things Will had to do to make himself ready. Things a woman didn't have to worry about.

Will got in the shower and scrubbed himself within an inch of his life. Then he set about working his fingers into himself, probing and stretching, so he didn't make a tit of himself when it came to taking Jack's cock.

Will's dick got hard as he stood under the spray. He tried to ignore it, then he blasted it with cold water, but his erection stayed, and he realized denying how much he wanted this was a waste of time.

He strapped his cock down with a towel and padded back to his bedroom. He half expected to find Jack asleep, or laughing his arse off at his big joke, but he found neither. Jack was awake and sitting up under the covers, hugging his knees to his chest.

"Did you change your mind?" Jack asked.

"Me?" Will opened a drawer and searched out some clean boxers. "No. I'm game if you are. How about you?"

"I want to. I'd feel better if you looked at me, though."

Will shut the drawer and gave Jack his full attention. Chanced a grin. "Happy?"

Jack smiled too. "I reckon so. Come here."

Will crawled onto the bed, underwear still clutched in his hand. Jack pried them free and tossed them aside. He glanced at the towel and frowned. "I'm naked under your duvet, so you should probably lose that too."

"Naked?" Will laughed. "What would you have done if I'd come back in and changed my mind?"

"Hoped you wouldn't notice?"

Fat chance of that. Will shucked his towel, turned the light off, and slid under the covers before he could start getting self-conscious.

They lay silent and still a moment, facing each other, staring. Then Will cleared his throat. "So, how do you want to do this? On top of me?"

"Don't blokes have to do it doggy style?"

Will studied Jack's face to see if he was serious, but in the dark he couldn't tell. "No, we can do it loads of ways, but if you want to pretend I'm a bird, we should probably stick to missionary."

They wriggled into position, Will on his back with Jack between his parted legs. If Jack felt weird about their half-hard cocks pressed together, he didn't let it show. He covered Will with his body and dropped his palms either side of his head. "I can kiss you, right? Like we did last time? I liked that."

In answer, Will hooked his hand around Jack's neck and tugged him down. Their lips met, hesitantly at first, but then, as the heat between them spread, their kisses became something more than they'd ever been. Lips, tongues, and teeth. It had been three years since that first kiss, and sometimes it felt like yesterday. Will thought the memory of their last encounter was seared on his soul, but he couldn't remember anything quite like this, and it wasn't long before he found himself arching up into Jack, grinding them together, grateful that Jack's tongue in his mouth prevented him from begging to be fucked.

Jack pulled away with a breathless grunt. "Have you got stuff?"

"Stuff?" Will fought for breath, his mind blank. "Yeah, shit. There's condoms and lube in the desk drawer."

Jack leaned across and fumbled around. He tossed a box of condoms on the bed and passed Will the lube like it was an unexploded bomb. "Where do you put that?"

"On me and on your dick." Will squeezed some onto his fingers. "Put a rubber on. I'll show you."

Will had decided in the shower that he wanted Jack to see as little of his arse as possible, but now, in the crazy heat of the moment, he didn't care so much. Jack sat back on his heels and fiddled with the condom. Will raised his legs, pressed his thighs to his chest, and lubed himself up.

It took him a moment to realize Jack was staring at his disappearing fingers, his eyes wide. "Does that hurt?"

"Nope. I like it. You ready?"

"Hmm? Oh, yeah. I think so." Jack edged closer, suddenly uncertain. "Show me what to do?"

Will shifted and aligned them, then he coaxed Jack forward. "This bit isn't like a girl. You've got to go slow, okay? In and out until you feel me relax inside."

Jack looked alarmed. Will rubbed his hip, but any more words of wisdom were cut off by the mind-blowing sensation of Jack's cock carefully nudging inside him.

Will shuddered; he couldn't help it. Jack was bigger than Dave—thicker, longer, and though it didn't hurt... yet, the slowly ratcheting pressure felt incredible. Intense.

Jack eased halfway in and his eyes bugged out. "Wow. That's so fucking tight. Feel like it's cutting the blood supply."

"That'll pass. Push in a bit more."

Jack obeyed and let Will guide him until he was all the way in. For a moment, neither of them spoke or moved. Will held his breath, waiting for the stinging burn of Jack inside him to fade or for Jack to freak out and leg it. Whichever came first.

But Jack didn't freak out. Instead, he raised his chest from Will's and rubbed Will's stomach. "You okay?"

Will blew out a few breaths. "I'm good. You can move now, if you want."

"Like this?" Jack rolled his hips in a slow, tentative circle. He gasped and his cheeks flushed.

Will gritted his teeth and felt sweat bead his brow. "Again."

Jack did it again and again, growing bolder with each pass. Then he dropped his head to Will's chest with a deep groan. "I'm gonna come so quick."

Will chuckled. "So? Not like you're trying to impress me, is it?"

Jack scowled. He pinched Will's nipple for good measure and seemed startled when Will moaned. "You like that?"

"Fuck, yeah." Will arched his back and resisted the urge to jack off. "Nipples are good. Pinching, sucking, biting. Come here. I'll show you."

Jack leaned down. Will palmed his chest and brushed his thumbs over Jack's nipples. Jack groaned. "Okay, you win. That rocks."

"Yeah? What about this?" Will grinned and clamped down on Jack's dick.

Jack yelped. "Don't do that. I'll blow."

"So blow." Will flexed his hips up. "Seriously. Do what you want. I want to watch."

Jack took a little persuasion, but eventually, he gave up trying to be cool and instead joined Will watching his cock slide in and out of Will's body. He seemed fascinated, and a dark blush crept over his chest. Then he grimaced and his whole body tightened, but his fight was futile. "Fuck. I'm gonna…."

He tensed and his mouth fell open in long silent moan. Will felt him pulse inside him and smiled. Jack was beautiful all the time, but flushed, slick with sweat, and blowing his load, he was the hottest thing Will had ever seen.

Jack's arms gave way. He collapsed on Will's chest, panting. Will held him. He wondered if he should say something, muss Jack's hair, or soothe him, but the moment passed as Jack softened and slipped out of him.

Will nudged him. "Get rid of the johnny, mate."

Jack roused himself and retrieved the condom. He tied a knot in it and fired it with perfect aim into Will's bedroom bin. He grinned a little, then frowned and brushed his hand over Will's still hard cock. "What about you?"

The touch was featherlight, but Will felt it everywhere. "Leave it. You might want to try again in a little while."

"Again?" Jack looked surprised, but he didn't move from the cradle of Will's parted legs. He seemed fascinated by Will's body.

So fascinated, Will squirmed under the scrutiny. "You've got your own ball bag, you know. Stop staring at mine."

"Hmm?" Jack glanced up. "Oh, sorry. I was just… um…."

"Yeah? Spit it out, mate. No point getting embarrassed now."

"Suppose not." Jack looked down, and to Will's toe-curling surprise, traced his entrance with his fingertip. "What's it called when you lick that?"

"Rimming… oh, fuck!" Will arched his back as Jack's tongue touched him, hesitant at first, but then with more purpose, circling and driving. "You don't have to… oh, oh, God, Jack."

Will braced himself on the bedframe. He'd tried this with Dave, but always, always the other way round. He'd never been on the receiving end, and God, it was good. So fucking good, Will had to wonder if Jack had done it before… or whether his theories about guys and girls being the same were actually true.

Not that it mattered. With Jack's tongue probing inside him, nothing mattered except the coil of pleasure twisting in his gut. Will let his body respond to Jack. He raised himself from the mattress and chased down the driving sweep of Jack's tongue, absorbing every thrusting lick until he felt he would burst.

Jack pulled back, grinning. He sat up and wiped his mouth. "That's fun. Never figured you for a screamer."

"Shut up...." Will caught sight of Jack's dick, and his retort died on his lips. Jack was hard again, hard and dripping. "Get another condom."

Jack grabbed the box and shook one out. Will grabbed it and rolled it onto Jack's cock. "Get on your back."

"My back?" Jack rolled over. He looked unsure, but Will had a plan. A plan he knew from experience would put a smile on Jack's face.

He straddled Jack and lowered himself slowly down on Jack's dick. Jack's face was a picture, and it didn't feel half-bad from the top either. He ground himself down on Jack, absorbing Jack's wide-eyed surprise. "Feel good?"

"Yeah." Jack reddened and that beautiful flush darkened his chest like it had never faded. "God, do that wiggly thing again."

Will obliged. He leaned back, angling his hips to meet Jack's tentative thrusts. It took a few tries, but then they met in the middle and found that magical place that made them both groan.

They didn't talk any more after that. The rhythm between them quickened and became urgent. The bed squeaked and juddered, then it banged into the wall again and again as heat boiled over into a frantic mess of grunts and slapping skin.

Jack didn't come quietly that time. He yelled and thrashed his head from side to side, dug his fingers into Will's thighs hard enough to leave bruises. Will watched it all through heavy eyes, pumping his hand over his cock. He'd told himself he wouldn't come on Jack, but by the time he remembered it was too late. He came with a groan and painted Jack's chest.

Will wiped the mess off Jack with a discarded T-shirt and tossed the condom, then collapsed in a heap on Jack, spaced and exhausted. Jack's fingers carding through his hair surprised him, but he couldn't bring himself to move. He'd never fucked Dave so hard… so intense, and he needed a minute.

A minute turned into five and then ten, and then Will realized he was falling asleep. He raised his head, searching for Jack. All he got was a smile and a gentle hand pushing him down.

"Go to sleep, mate. You rocked my world."

CHAPTER THREE

SEPTEMBER 18

10:30 p.m.

Will: *So… is this how we're going to talk now? I tried your phone a few times, but it didn't connect. Guess your international plan didn't work or something. How are things going in sunny Ibiza? Did you have a good summer? What have you been up to???*

December 29

04:45 a.m.

Jack: *So you do know how to e-mail?*

Sorry it's taken so long to reply. Didn't know how to get into this in-box. Forgot my password was your bloody birthday. Remember when we set that up?

Anyway, things have been craaaaaazy here. Summer was mental. I blinked and it was over. I had a plan to stick around and get a bar job until I got another DJ gig, but the head honcho from Café Mambo came to see me play on my last day. He offered me an off-peak slot until spring, so I took it. Looks like I'll be here until April at least, maybe longer if I can impress some more club owners.

How's Leeds? Tell me everything. Feels proper weird knowing you're up there and not at home. Have you been out on the pull? Bet you have…

January 3
    06:00 a.m.
    Jack: *Will? You there?*

January 5
    11:00 p.m.
    Will: *Are you taking the piss? I don't want to know why you're awake at 6:00 a.m. do I? STILL awake, I bet.*

    Thanks for your e-mail, mate. Sounds like you're having the time of your life. Not surprised it took you THREE MONTHS to get back to me. Can't believe Café Mambo head-hunted you. That's so fucking cool! That place is more commercial than where you were before, right? What are you going to play? Are you gonna dip into the dark side and mix some house tunes?

    Leeds is all good. My flat's a bit grotty, but I'm moving into a house with a bunch of girls next year so it's not so bad. You'd like them actually… the girls, that is. Leeds is full of them. The ratio is, like, 3:1. If I was straight, I'd have no excuse for being single. Cause, yeah. In answer to your subtle (not) question. I am still single. There's some really cool clubs around here and I've hooked up with a few blokes, but nothing serious.

    Oh, hey… if you're taking on a new residency, when are you coming back to the UK? Your mum really missed you at Christmas. Think she had one too many port and lemons, 'cause she was chatting up my dad. (FYI: I had to bleach my ears after that.) Speak soon, mate

February 2
    06:00 a.m.
    Jack: *Did you seriously put a smiley face on the end of that e-*

mail? (And yeah, I DO know you sent it a month ago. Things have been mental)

Glad you're still loving Leeds. And score for the girls. Bet they smell way better than a flat full of blokes. I've met a few birds, but like you... nothing serious. Haven't got the time, you know? When I'm not playing I'm mixing or producing... or trying to get some fucking sleep. This island is crazy, man. It's alive all night, then I feel weird about sleeping the day away when the sun is so bright. Feel like I should make the most of it.

My apartment is wicked. There's a studio in the basement. I'm thinking of producing my own tracks. You're right about Café Mambo being commercial. I can play the stuff they like, but those dirty beats we used to mix in that field in Surrey suit me better. Miss those days sometimes. Hey, you should come over. You get holidays, right?

February 5

09:45 p.m.

Will: *Hey, Jack. Yeah, I get holidays, but I'm a poor student, remember? I can't afford the bus to the library, let alone a bloody flight. Thanks for the invite, though. Maybe after uni, if you're still there.*

FYI: I quite like the smell of sweaty men.

February 11

07:00 a.m.

Jack: *Dude, I'd pay for your flight, and you'd be staying with me, so it would be free. Come over. Please?*

09:30 a.m.

Will: *Maybe next year. Are you coming home at all before summer? Maybe we could hit Glasto or something?*

. . .

February 17

11:00 p.m.

Will: *Helloooo? Jack? You there?*

March 1

10:30 p.m.

Will: *I take it you died and no one told me….*

March 5

08:45 a.m.

Jack: *All right, all right. You're worse than my mum, you know that? Sorry, mate. Been busy. I'm not at Café Mambo anymore. I got a gig at Pacha instead, five days a week, midnight till four, then I play at Insomniacs down the road until 8:00 a.m.*

It's crazy, but I like it. I've been doing some producing too. Signed a deal with XS to mix a compilation album for them. Should be out late this year. You'd better buy it!

So… when are you gonna come over? You can bring some mates, if you want. I checked the flight prices. It's only fifty quid out of Luton.

10:00 a.m.

Will: *I live in Leeds, remember?*

March 8

08:30 a.m.

Jack: *Okay, Leeds, then. Same price. Why are you being a dick? If you don't want to come, just say so….*

01:30 p.m.

Will: *Jack, I'm not being a dick, I'm just skint. I'm really*

pleased you signed a production deal, but some of us are living on
Pot Noodle.

March 10
03:00 a.m.

Will: *Okay, maybe I am being a dick. I'm sorry. I DO want to come and see you, but it's going to take some planning. I've got a job at the local gay bar (all rainbows and glitter, you'd love it). If I can save some spending money I'll come over at the end of term.*

09:00 a.m.

Jack: *Really? I'd like that. I miss you.*

09:15 a.m.

Will: *Not doing drugs, are you?*

10:00 p.m.

Will: *Jack????*

March 12
08:15 a.m.

Jack: *LOL. NO. I'm not doing drugs. Just a bit of weed to help me sleep after a crazy gig. Though if I wanted to do other shit, I wouldn't have to look far. I meant it, though. I do miss you. No one gets me like you do.*

08:30 a.m.

Will: *Piss off, you soppy date. I'm just getting up, so I know you're just getting in. Go to sleep, mate.*

• • •

08:35 a.m.

Jack: *K.*

May 11

02:30 p.m.

Will: *So, I booked my flight… July 30. Three days of fun in the sun. Hope you're ready for a crowd of rowdy northerners. It's okay for me to bring a couple of people, right? 'Cause once I showed that picture in* Mixmag *to my friends, they all want to come. Did you know you're famous now?*

May 12

08:47 a.m.

Jack: *You booked your flight? Nice one. 'Bout fucking time. And yeah, bring whoever you want. I've got a couple of spare beds and a couch. We'll figure it out. Let me know the times. I'll meet you at the airport if I can.*

And fuck Mixmag. *They called my stuff "grungy house". WTF? Don't buy that mag again. Ever.*

11:00 a.m.

Will: *Yes, dear.*

May 2003

Leeds. England.

WILL SHUT his laptop with the rueful frown he always found plastered on his face when communication with Jack went well… when Jack responded to an e-mail before so much time lapsed that Will forgot what they'd been talking about. The familiar banter—albeit strained by a separation Will was still getting used to—reminded him why he bothered, something that proved difficult whenever Will recalled the day he'd stood on Jack's doorstep and waited for a good-bye that had never come….

"Earth to Will?"

Will blinked. Suki, his housemate, waved her hand in front of his face. "Hmm? Sorry. Didn't hear you come in."

Suki snorted. "So I see. Who are you daydreaming about? That hot accountant bloke again?"

"Evan? Fuck, no. I was thinking about our big summer trip, actually. I just told Jack we booked our flights."

"Oooh. Get in! What did he say? Is he really cool with you bringing a bunch of girls to stay at his place?"

"Seems to be." Will shrugged, though with Jack it was sometimes hard to tell. His e-mails fluctuated between total word vomit and nothing at all. "And he likes girls, so I'm sure he'll be fine with you all taking over his place."

Suki hummed. "I keep forgetting he's straight. How long have you known him again?"

Will sloshed water into two mugs already loaded with tea bags, milk, and sugar. "Most of my life. He moved into the house next door a week after my mum died. I was six, I think, and he'd just turned seven."

"That's nice." Suki hopped up onto the counter and claimed her tea. Will ruffled her spiky pink hair. She was his favorite flatmate, and he was looking forward to sharing an actual house with her next year. "He does know you're gay, right? I mean, my cousin didn't tell his mates back home for years. Couldn't face it, even though he was out and proud up here."

Will winced. He heard shit like that all the time, and it always reminded him how lucky he'd been with his dad and Jack. "He was the first person I ever told, actually. In fact, I think he knew before I did."

"And he was all right with it? I don't want to judge, but he looks like a bit of a lad. Doesn't it ever get awkward?"

Will chuckled. All of Suki's friends had gone gaga over

Jack's picture in the music magazine, and he couldn't blame them. Life in the sunshine suited Jack. With his tanned, sculpted arms, he'd never looked hotter. "He was fine. Nothing bothers him. Reckon I could've told him I wanted a sex change and he wouldn't have blinked."

Bet he wouldn't have shagged you, though.

Will hid his flush in his cup of tea. Thinking about *that* night often gave him a strange feeling inside. Stranger, even, than waking up naked in bed with Jack, both of them still sticky from the night before. That particular morning had felt oddly normal, but the days that followed had been weird —*Jack* had been weird. Will had wondered if he regretted what had happened between them. Not that Jack had been around to tell him, and when he'd ditched Will in favor of footie practice the morning Will was due to decamp to Leeds, Will had taken that as a sign: Jack was done, in more ways than one.

Hadn't stopped him scrawling Jack a soppy note and leaving the crumpled pages with Jack's dad, though. Will winced when he thought about it, but Jack hadn't mentioned it, and perhaps he never would.

Will could only hope.

They hadn't set eyes on each other since. These days they kept in contact when their conflicting schedules allowed, mainly e-mail and the occasional phone call. Will often thought of Jack late at night when he was going to bed, tapping out an e-mail last thing before he fell asleep. Jack's replies were usually posted first thing in the morning, but Will was under no illusions that Jack was just getting up. No. By the sounds of things, Jack was hardly sleeping at all.

Suki punched his arm. "You always do that when we talk about him."

"Ow!" Will rubbed his arm. "Do what who now?"

Suki laughed. "Jack… your straight friend. Talking about him always sends you to another planet. What's up with that?"

Will scowled. "Nothing. I wasn't thinking about Jack, if you must know. I was *thinking* about the hot accountant guy your mate set me up with."

The lie came easily. Will was used to hiding his feelings for Jack. He'd done it his whole life.

Suki's face brightened. "Are you going to see him again?"

Will forced his mind into the present and pictured the slim, fiercely intelligent redhead he'd shared a KFC with the night before. Evan Lewis was great—sharp, funny and gorgeous. They'd had a lot of fun, and the sweet kiss they'd shared after was almost the hottest kiss Will had ever had.

Almost.

"Sure," Will said. "He's going to the Wendy House on Saturday. I said I'd meet him there. You'll come with me, won't you?"

"To the Wendy House?" Suki jumped down from the counter and swiped Will's packet of custard creams. "Try and stop me. And who knows? If things go well, you can invite Evan to Ibiza with us. I'm sure *Jack* can find room for one more."

Suki danced off with Will's biscuits before he could think of a suitable answer. He watched her go, pondering, still clutching his tea. He hardly knew Evan, but the thought of taking him to Ibiza… to visit Jack… felt all wrong. It was a stupid idea, wasn't it?

A MONTH or so later, Will found himself slowly changing his mind. If the pictures in the music magazines were to be believed, Jack probably wouldn't notice if Will turned up with his long-dead mother hanging off his arm. Clubs, models, groupies. Jack was fast becoming a superstar on the DJ circuit, and so much had changed Will had to wonder if they'd even recognize each other.

Besides, things with Evan had moved on too….

Will rolled over. There wasn't much room in the single bed, but Will followed the natural curve of Evan's body and drove inside him again, searching out that sweet, textured knot that made Evan curse and chew a hole in the pillow.

Beneath him, Evan rose up on all fours. He pushed back onto Will and urged him on. "Harder. Do it. I won't bloody break."

Will gave in and slammed Evan into the mattress, though he caught himself inwardly rolling his eyes. Evan liked it a little rough, and though Will enjoyed it well enough, something about it sometimes felt a little forced, like they were performing for a crowd who didn't much care.

Didn't stop him getting off, mind. Even now, when his thoughts were elsewhere. He pulled out of Evan and collapsed in a heap beside him. He lay still a moment, panting, before he set about a halfhearted cleanup.

Evan rolled over when he was done and put his chin on his chest. "You seem miles away today. Everything okay?"

"Miles away?" Will quirked an eyebrow. "We seem pretty close to me."

"Very funny. You want me to bottom worship you? Tell you what a monster top you are?"

"Piss off. I'm right here. Maybe it's you who's distracted." Will gave Evan a playful shove. Topping was a relatively new experience for him, but one he'd found he was good at if the few blokes he'd tried it with were to be believed.

Evan hummed softly. "Maybe. I've been thinking about the summer break. A few of my mates are going to Barcelona for a few weeks. Do you want to come?"

Ah. Will had known that was coming. Evan had been dropping hints for weeks and Will had been doing the same, hoping to let him know it wasn't going to happen without having a fuck-awkward conversation. Seemed he should've tried harder. "Sorry. I'm already going to Ibiza. I can't afford two trips."

"Ibiza? You never said."

"Didn't I?" Now that *was* news to Will. At home, the impending trip was all he and his flatmates ever talked about, but then he didn't often bring Evan home, choosing instead to fuck and kip at Evan's place in Beeston.

Evan nudged him. "No, you didn't. Who are you going to Ibiza with?"

"Suki and the girls. I have a friend who DJs out there. We're staying with him."

"Oh."

Evan didn't say anymore, and it was a while before Will began to feel bad. He looked down at Evan and pictured the image he'd seen of Jack just that morning, plastered all over a tacky white couch with girls all over him. Lately, those images had come to replace the ones Will carried close to his heart. The ones of Jack naked and writhing beneath him….

Stop it. He's straight, remember?

"Come with us, if you want?"

Evan glanced up. He looked startled enough for Will to wonder how long it had been since either of them had spoken. "To Ibiza with you?"

Will shrugged. "Jack said I can bring who I want and the flights are only fifty quid."

"Do you want me to come?"

"If you like." Will forced himself not to shrug again. He and Evan weren't exactly boyfriends, but they'd moved past the friends-with-benefits stage, and Will liked Evan, most of the time. They got on well enough and the sex was… great. Why not take it to the next level? To another bloody country and see how it went?

"Why not? It'll be fun."

CHAPTER FOUR

July 2003

Ibiza

WILL AND his five partners in crime—four girls and Evan —piled off the plane into a hazy wall of sunshine. Will stumbled, already half-pissed from the flight and hanging around the airport, and the heat hit him like a shot of cheap Sambuca.

Evan caught him and grinned. "Easy, babe."

Will righted himself and resisted the urge to roll his eyes. Evan had started calling him *babe* one night after Will had drunk too much blue vodka at a rowdy flat party. Will hated it, but after puking on Evan's favorite shoes, he hadn't had the heart to tell him to shut the fuck up.

Suki poked Will's arm. "Come on. Let's get our bags so we can find your superhot DJ friend."

They made their way through the busy airport, hyper and loud, but this was Ibiza and no one seemed to care. Will grabbed his bag from the luggage carousel. He wandered to a bench to wait for the others.

Evan joined him a few moments later. "You didn't tell me your friend was hot."

"He's straight. Why would I?"

"Why not?" Evan shrugged. "Lila told me he's famous. How come I've never heard of him?"

"Erm, because you like cheesy pop music? Jack plays drum-and-bass and techno trance, or he used to. I'm not sure what he plays over here."

Evan looked mystified, but that wasn't unusual. Aside from being gay lads from the southeast of England and sharing some half-decent sexual chemistry, he and Will didn't have much in common.

Suki and her crazy pals, Lila, Jo, and Cara, found their way to the bench. Will looked at them and shook his head. Pink hair, tattoos, and enough piercings to make a grown man shudder. He wondered what Jack would make of them. They weren't anything like the girls they'd known back home.

Jo tugged Will's sleeve. "Where are we meeting the superhot DJ?"

Will scowled. Why did everyone keep saying that? "He said he'd wait out front. His place is a ten-minute walk away."

They shouldered their bags and pushed their way through the airport. Will felt a shot of nerves as they jostled through the tourists and natives. He hadn't seen Jack for the better part of a year. What if he didn't recognize him? Or, worse, what if they didn't like each other anymore? Jack had been his best friend for as long as he could remember, but the distance between them now had begun to feel horribly normal.

They made it outside. Will looked beyond the rows of waiting cars and taxis, searching for a mop of sandy hair. For a moment he came up blank and his stomach did an odd flip. Jack wasn't there. Then he found his gaze suddenly locked in the dark liquid haze he knew so well and his companions faded away. Will dropped his bag and crossed the street. Jack met him halfway and wrapped him in a bear hug, a warm, tight embrace that, even in the middle of the blazing Mediterranean, felt like home.

Jack slapped Will's back. "It's good to see you, man. How was the flight? I forgot until this morning you'd never been on a plane before."

"It was fine." Will mumbled the words into the scrap of a vest Jack was almost wearing, unwilling to let go until he remembered they were blocking the road. For a moment, they stared at each other, wide-eyed and giddy. Jack looked amazing—tanned and healthy, his hair streaked with sun-lightened blond. Will drank him in. Wow. Had he always been this hot?

Jack punched his arm. "Look at you. Your hair's so long."

Will fingered the ends of his light blond chin-length hair. In recent months, he'd lacked the inclination and funds to get it cut. The girls said he looked like a green-eyed Kurt Cobain with it long, but Will figured they were looking for a kind way to tell him he was skinny and pale. "I had a beard a few weeks ago, but it turned ginger so I shaved it off."

Jack laughed and his grin matched the sun. "Take a picture next time. I need evidence."

"Arsehole."

"Yep. So… where are your friends?"

"My friends? Shit." Will had all but forgotten Evan, Suki, and the girls waiting for him on the other side of the road. "They're over there."

Jack followed Will's gaze and his eyebrows shot up in surprise. He waved. The girls looked excited, and Evan… fuck, *Evan*. Jack had been hard to pin down recently, and Will had never got round to telling him Evan was coming.

Will opened his mouth to explain, but Jack was already crossing the road.

The girls swarmed around him. Jack hugged them all before he extended his hand to Evan. "All right, mate? I'm Jack."

"So I see." Evan shook Jack's hand. "I'm Evan, Will's boyfriend."

Evan said it with a smile, but for some reason Will wanted

the ground to swallow him up. They'd been sleeping together and socializing for a few months, but boyfriends? Really? The term made Will cringe.

If Jack was surprised, he didn't let it show. Instead he took Cara's bag from her—the biggest, by miles—and pointed to an apartment block on the beachfront. "My place is this way. Come on. I'll show you."

The walk to Jack's apartment felt odd. The girls talked a mile a minute, mainly at Jack, but Evan didn't say a word, Will either, and though he was the glue tying them all together, he felt strangely detached, like he was storing it all to watch later.

Perhaps it was Jack's back. The whole walk, Will couldn't stop staring at it. Jack had always been fit and athletic, not too huge, but he seemed leaner now... in a good way, like he'd lost the soft, innocent curves leftover from childhood. His profile was sharper now, angled, and his back was a bloody wet dream.

Evan nudged Will. "That's the last time I buy you a double vodka. You look like you need a nap."

Jack glanced over his shoulder. "Will can't drink in daylight. Makes him sleepy."

Will rolled his eyes. Daytime drinking had always been his undoing. How many times had he fallen asleep on Jack in the park? "It's not the vodka. It's the three pints of Stella I drank for breakfast. And anyway, it's the first time you've bought me anything but pissy Foster's from the union."

That shut Evan up, though it was Jack who frowned. Despite being an accountant, Evan was shit with money, and by the end of each month it was always Will who ended up buying the drinks. Not that he minded much. Evan was a lightweight. It didn't take much to put him on his arse, and Evan was at his most fun when three sheets to the wind.

Will's dirty thoughts cut off as Jack's apartment block appeared in front of him. From the outside it looked pretty plain, but Will realized his mistake as soon as they got inside.

With its sleek, modern interior and prime beach views, the place was a palace. "Wow. This looks like *MTV Cribs*."

Jack chuckled. "Nice, eh? It's a lot better than the first place I had when I came out here. Back then I just had a mattress at the back of the club. This place comes with the job at Pacha. I share it with some guys, but they're in Ayia Napa this week."

He rattled off some names. Will shook his head. *Some guys?* Bollocks. Jack was sharing a house with a bunch of living legends, in the DJ world at least. Even Evan had heard of them. Will pondered what that meant for Jack. He knew Jack was rising fast and, by the look of him, having the time of his life. Did that mean Will's fears that Jack would never come home were going to come true? Was this it now? Annual visits in the sunshine with a crowd of onlookers along for the ride? Will had spent a year convincing himself it was as it should be, but faced with it now, it didn't feel right. Nothing did.

Will sidestepped Evan's reaching hand and picked up his bag. "Where are we sleeping?"

Jack blinked, and Will realized he'd been staring while Will had been lost in thought. "This way."

Jack's apartment had three bedrooms. The girls took two between them, leaving one room—Jack's room—left. Jack opened the door. Will poked his head in. For Jack, it was surprisingly tidy and minimalist, just a bed, a sound system, and a chest of drawers.

"You two can, uh, sleep in here," Jack said. "I'll take the couch."

"You don't have to sleep on the couch," Will protested. "It's your place."

Jack shrugged. "I'm easy. There's only one of me. Besides, it'll be like the old days."

"Yeah, the prehistoric old days."

Evan trod on Will's foot. "Leave him alone. He's already said he's hardly ever here."

Had he? Will didn't remember that, but then he hadn't taken much notice of the conversations Jack had been having with anyone else.

Evan took Will's silence as acquiescence and dumped his bag on Jack's bed. "Can I use your shower? I feel totally minging from the flight."

"Sure." Jack inclined his head down the hall. "Bathroom's that way."

"Cheers, mate." Evan gathered his toiletries, kissed Will's cheek, and disappeared, leaving Will and Jack alone for the first time since last summer.

"So...."

"So." Will sat on the edge of Jack's bed, deflated. He'd been desperate to see Jack for months, craving the easy friendship he'd missed so much, but it all felt weird now. Like a belated cloud of awkwardness had caught up with them.

"Evan seems... nice. You didn't tell me you were seeing someone."

Will shrugged. "It's kinda casual. He didn't decide he was definitely coming until a few weeks ago. Sorry I didn't tell you. It slipped my mind."

"It's cool. I said bring who you want." Jack leaned casually on the doorframe. It didn't escape Will's notice that he seemed reluctant to venture further into his own room. "What are you up to tonight? Anything good?"

"The girls want to hit the beach, but other than that, not really." Will stretched his arms over his head. "Think we're going to save ourselves for tomorrow."

Jack grinned. "You're coming to Pacha tomorrow, right? Write your friends' names down for me. I'll put them on the guest list."

"Guest list, eh? Does that mean we get in for free?"

"Yep. No queuing, either. And you get access to more of the club. Be easier for me to find you. That place gets crazy."

Will would have to take Jack's word for it. The sort of clubs he went to in Leeds were nothing like the cool, slick clubs of Ibiza, and part of him wondered what he was letting himself in for.

"Anyway." Jack pushed himself off the doorframe in a languid, fluid movement. "I've gotta get to work. I'll see you tomorrow, yeah?"

"What?" Will sat up. "You're not staying? I thought you were off tonight."

"Caught a last-minute gig at Dragon Ball. It's a tough place to get into. Can't really say no."

"Dragon Ball? Is that the secret party network I read about in *Mixmag*?"

Jack grinned. "Probably, but I told you not to read that shit anymore. I'd take you along, but it's a pretty heavy night. I think some of your girls could take it, but I don't reckon your boyfriend would like it. Down and dirty, you know? Like old times."

Old times. That bloody phrase again. What was it about those two little words that cut Will to the bone? Maybe it was because he knew Jack was right. Suki would love a dirty stomping rave, especially one in the mystical heat of Ibiza, but the others, not so much. And Evan? No fucking chance. The bloke was dirty in bed, but that's where it stayed.

Will sighed. "So you won't be back until the morning?"

"Probably not." Jack looked as though he might just walk away, but then he echoed Will's soft sigh and crossed the room. He bent down and squeezed Will into another tight bear hug. "It's good to see you, mate. I've missed you."

He left before Will could reply.

I missed you too.

WILL ROLLED over in bed. His face collided with Evan's back and he wrinkled his nose. Evan smelled sweet, like the bubblegum mojitos he'd been drinking all day, and combined with the warm breeze blowing through the open window, it wasn't a scent Will enjoyed.

He shifted again with a heavy sigh. Two hours had passed since they'd stumbled back to Jack's deserted apartment, and he was still wide-awake... wide-awake and in denial that he was waiting for Jack to come home.

Yeah, 'cause that wasn't pathetic at all.

A noise in the hallway disturbed the sullen quiet of the night—scrabbling and a soft thud. Will figured it was the girls still messing around, until he heard a decidedly masculine grunt. He glanced at Evan. There were no other blokes due home to the apartment, so that had to be Jack, right?

With another sigh, Will heaved himself out of bed. He wasn't sleeping anyway, and his curiosity was driving him up the bloody wall.

He crept across the room. Evan looked out for the count, but Will felt so restless he couldn't imagine his tiptoeing footsteps not waking the whole world. He slipped into the hallway and found it empty. He followed the sound of muffled voices to the living room and absorbed the scene slowly, like a bad, drunken dream.

The Mediterranean heat ran from Will's blood. Jack was standing by the couch, shorts round his ankles and his dick in the mouth of a naked woman. In the soft light of the early morning, Will could see she was stunning, all long shimmery limbs and perfect boobs. Jack pulled her up and bent her over the arm of the couch. He turned his head and the first glimmers of the rising sun caught his face: eyes blank, lips curled in a snarl.

Will's stomach turned over. He felt like he might faint, but he made it to the bathroom in time to lose a whole day of beer and deep-fried calamari. After, he crept back to Jack's room and shut the door with a quiet click. He lay back on the sheets that smelled of Jack, heart pounding, though he didn't know why. He'd seen Jack with girls more times than he could count, so why the fuck was he puking? Perhaps it was shock. He'd been in Ibiza for fifteen hours and he didn't feel like he'd seen Jack at all. Still felt like he hadn't seen his best friend for nearly a year, and the yearning ache in his belly remained.

Will closed his eyes and searched for a positive. The day had passed in a haze of sunbathing, drinking, and sightseeing. Will had been ambivalent toward the crowds of bikini-clad girls, but he'd fallen in love with the vibrant street artists who performed on every corner—dancers, magicians, fire-eaters. Will had been captivated, and he'd fallen into bed—Jack's bed—feeling bewitched and inspired. Now he felt like he could scratch his eyes out, bleach his retinas, and still see the look on Jack's face as he drove his cock into that beautiful girl. So much for looking on the bright side.

There was no fucking way he was going back to sleep anytime soon. Instead, he lay awake, taunted by Evan's steady breaths, and tried to reconcile what he'd seen tonight with the memories of Jack he held so dear. He remembered the moment Jack had awkwardly pushed inside him like it was yesterday. Remembered Jack's soft look of wonder and gentle caress of Will's stomach. Was that the same man screwing a chick blind in the next room? Who the hell knew? Not Will. Maybe his memories were hopelessly skewed, hanging on to shit that wasn't real. Jack was straight, he always had been, and their encounter had been a one-off, an experiment.

So get the fuck over it.

Despite his fretting, Will eventually fell asleep, and he woke a few hours later, sweating, to an empty bed. He sat up and pushed his damp hair behind his ears. The sun was streaming through the open window, and outside he could hear the party island was already in full swing.

Will hauled himself out of bed and into the shower. Once he'd dressed in Bermuda shorts and a T-shirt, he ventured to the kitchen, bypassing the living room, and found Evan at the table, flipping through the stacks of DJ publications that littered every room of the apartment.

Evan waved a magazine in greeting. "What the hell is psych-tech-dub-trance?"

Will shrugged and opened the cupboards, searching for glasses. "Fucked if I know. Are the girls up?"

"Not yet. It's only nine o'clock. Suki was trashed last night. Don't think she'll be up before noon."

Will chuckled. "That's optimistic. She'll have her head in the bog before she sees daylight. Spirits don't agree with her."

"Hmm. She might have already done that. I'm sure I heard someone blowing chunks last night. What about you? Sore head? You were thrashing around most of the night."

"Was I?" That was news to Will. Last thing he remembered, Evan had been oblivious to Will's Jack-induced torment beside him. Maybe he hadn't been as KO'd as Will thought. "Must've got too hot."

Evan shrugged. "Yeah, you'd think they'd have air-con in a place like this, wouldn't you? Jack told me there's a recording studio beneath this building. Why would you build all that and not put even a bloody fan up here?"

Jack told me. "When did you speak to Jack?"

"This morning. He came home as I got up. That's why I'm holed up in here. He's asleep on the couch."

"Oh." Will finally found a glass, opened the fridge, and retrieved the Ribena they'd bought the day before. He mixed a big glass and chugged it down. "Did he say anything else?"

"Who?"

"*Jack.*"

"*Jack* didn't say much." Evan eyed Will over the rim of his own glass of squash. "He looked even more hungover than you, if such a thing is possible. Maybe you should stay out of the sun today."

"Piss off." Will scowled and stomped away to the apartment's beachfront balcony. He leaned on the railing and stared out beyond the crowded white sand to the sea. Until twenty-four hours ago, coming to see Jack in Ibiza had felt like a dream, but now he was wondering if he'd made the biggest mistake of his life.

WILL KNEW the moment Jack took control of the DJ stage. He'd spent much of the past decade watching Jack mix and make music, and though Pacha was a world away from the grimy underground raves back in England, Will *knew*. Jack had a style… a certain magic when he hit the decks, and Will would recognize it anywhere.

Not that he could see any more of Jack than the top of his head. Despite the VIP passes, Pacha was jam-packed.

"Are you going to stare at him all night?"

"What?" Will glared at Evan, irritated.

Evan arched an eyebrow. "Don't give me 'what'. You've been following his every move since we got here and staring at him for the last two hours."

Part of Will was surprised it had taken Evan so long to notice his pathetic preoccupation with Jack, but on the surface he was bloody annoyed. "Piss off. I *came* here to see him play. It's not unreasonable for me to look at him."

"And the rest."

Evan's tone caught Suki's attention. She danced over and inserted herself between Will and Evan. "No squabbling on holiday. Will, you might want to rescue your friend. I saw Cara heading to the DJ's cool-down room. Poor Jack's gonna walk right into her clutches when he comes off stage."

Shit. Will's skin crawled. Cara was a nice enough girl to share a bathroom with, but she went through men like hot dinners, and despite what he'd seen last night, Will didn't want her anywhere near Jack.

Will abandoned Evan and pushed his way through the club. He knew he was being a dick to Evan, but the bloke was driving Will mental with his bitching and sniping. Was it any wonder Will hadn't wanted to fuck him in Jack's bed when they'd stumbled home for a siesta that afternoon?

Yeah, 'cause the fact that Jack was still asleep in the next room had nothing to do with it....

Will tried to ignore the monster in his head and maneuvered his way through the sweaty crowds. He waved his pink wristband at the bouncer guarding the door to the DJ's room and hustled his way inside.

The room was quieter than the rest of the club, and the drop in volume disoriented Will for a moment. He stopped and searched out his bearings. The lights were muted, and each dark corner was kitted out with low-lying couches and beanbags. Most of them were occupied, and it didn't take Will long to find Jack and Cara all over each other. He considered leaving them to it. The chill-out room had the kind of vibe that suggested no one would care if someone was shagging in the corner, but something stopped him. Fuck's sake, he'd traveled a thousand miles to see Jack, and they were flying out the next morning. Will didn't want to leave with Jack's conquests and fighting with Evan his only bloody memories.

Will kicked Jack's legs, gleaning little satisfaction from the surprise in his face. He focused on Cara. "Suki's looking for you."

"So?" Cara kept her attention on Jack. "She'll find me if it's important."

"It is important." Will fought to keep his tone even, to keep from grabbing Cara and yanking her away from Jack. "She said to meet her in the toilets downstairs."

Cara still looked as though she might protest. Jack nudged her. "Go on. Don't leave your mates hanging. I'll find you later."

The promise seemed to mollify Cara. She disentangled herself and disappeared into thin air. At least, that's what it felt like. Will didn't watch her go, and neither did Jack.

"What's up, mate?"

"Nothing's up,"

"Yeah? So why did you just lie through your teeth to get rid of that bird?"

"What makes you think I was lying?" Will finally looked at Jack. Took in his bright eyes, flushed skin, and tousled hair.

Jack reached behind the couch and retrieved a bottle of water. "How many times have I watched you bullshit your dad, eh? Tell him we're going night fishing instead of raving at Junction 14? What's the matter?"

It was the first time Jack had really looked at Will since their reunion on the pavement outside the airport, a reunion that felt like a dream, cooked up by Will's overactive imagination. "Nothing's the matter."

"Bollocks." Jack twisted the cap onto his water bottle. Then he stood and gripped Will's arm. "Come on. Let's chip this joint."

WILL FOLLOWED Jack up the steep stone steps carved into the cliff face. "Where are we going?"

"You'll see."

Jack continued his ascent of the cliff. Will grumbled. He didn't like heights, and the climb seemed to go on forever until he walked right into Jack's back.

Jack chuckled. "Easy. Hold on to me until we get round this corner, and don't look down."

As if. Will had made the plane ride over buoyed by a skinful and the tingling anticipation of seeing Jack. Climbing a cliff in the dark was his idea of hell, and Jack was the only soul on earth who could coax him to do it. He held on for dear life as Jack guided them around the uneven cliff, gaze fixed on Jack's neck, trying to ignore the sound of crumbling rock and the waves crashing somewhere below. "I fucking hate you. You know that, don't you?"

"Stop whinging." Jack took another few steps, then let out

a breath. "Okay, lean back against the rock. That's it. Now sit down and open your eyes."

"They are open." But as Will followed Jack's instruction, slid down the bumpy rock to sit on his arse, and looked out over the horizon, he realized how misguided those three little words really were.

Bloody hell. The view was like nothing Will had ever seen before. The sun was beginning to rise, glittering off the sea, and high up in the cliffs, nestled in a sheltered ledge, watching it all unfold, Will felt like Jack had brought him to the top of the world.

"It looks like Narnia, that bit when they get crowned at the end."

Jack bumped Will's shoulder. "I thought that when I first came up here. Made me think of you. Hope you're not too pissed to make it down without breaking your neck."

"You won't let me fall." Will didn't want to consider the perilous climb down just yet, but he knew it was true. Jack had always been the one between Will and a hard place. Always.

Jack fell quiet for a while, perhaps watching, amused, as Will stared at the view in wonder. Will stretched his legs out in front of him. The ledge was wide and deep, and despite the height, he felt perfectly safe. Safe enough to slump into Jack and dump his head on his shoulder. Huh. Perhaps he was drunker than he thought.

Jack didn't seem to notice, and his deep, even breathing was like a metronome until he broke the quiet. "How long have you been with that prat Evan?"

Will reluctantly lifted his head. "Why do you think he's a prat?"

"Because he talks about you like you're an idiot."

"How so?"

"Does it matter?"

Probably not. Will toed off his shoes and set about rolling

up his jeans. "I haven't been seeing him long. A few months, maybe? It's nothing serious."

"He told me you were moving in together next year."

Will pulled a face. "That's bollocks. I'm renting a house with Suki and the girls. Did he really say that? Bloody hell. He was only supposed to be a fuck buddy."

Jack chuckled. "Well, you should probably tell him that before he picks out your wedding china."

"Piss off." Will thought about shoving Jack, but the drop below put him off, and anyway, it felt good to be teased by Jack again. He'd missed Jack's gentle ribbing. "I'll sort him out when we get home. How about you? Sowing your wild oats?"

Jack was silent a moment, engrossed with carving his initials into the stone ledge. "I've had some fun. You were right, though. About girls, I mean."

"Was I?" Will was mystified. When had he ever given Jack advice on girls?

"Yeah." Jack abandoned his stone sketch and stared out at the sea. "You said it wasn't the same, and it's not."

Oh. Will didn't know what to say. He watched Jack light a cigarette and waved his proffered pack away. "Gave up. Could only afford roll-ups and they're minging."

Jack processed this with an absent nod. He sat back and tilted his face to the sky, leaning on Will the way he used to when he blew smoke to the moon from Will's bedroom window.

Will leaned back on the cliff wall, half-asleep, and absorbed the warmth of the sun. The air between him and Jack felt heavy and unresolved, but in the heady heat of an early morning, far from home, he couldn't make himself fret. After all, he'd be home in twenty-four hours, leaving Jack still here, bonking every girl who smiled at him and flashed her boobs, and what the hell was wrong with that?

However Will felt, Jack was just his mate, right?

CHAPTER FIVE

OCTOBER 1

02:30 a.m.

Jack: *Hey, goldilocks, long time no speak. Twenty-nine days. That's gotta be a record, right? Anyway, I know you're probably out partying with Evan, and I've got be quick as I'm pinching the club's internet, but can you call the number I gave you when you've got a minute? I need a favor. Ta.*

12:04 p.m.

Will: *FYI: I was out partying, but NOT with EVAN. We split up. And FYI again, I've called that bloody number a million times in the past year and IT DOESN'T WORK. If you want to talk to me, you'll have to call me yourself.*

October 5

10:15 p.m.

Jack: *I did call you. No one ever answers the phone in your house. Can't you get a mobile like the rest of the world? P.S. Sorry about Evan. I thought he was a knobber, but you must've liked him to stay with him, so… yeah. Sorry.*

. . .

October 10

10:30 a.m.

Will: *The rest of the world? Student, remember? I might pick up a pay-as-you-go next month when I get paid, but I doubt it will take international calls without eating my credit, so….*

If you want me, you'll have to sit your arse down and type it out.

October 19

09:15 a.m.

Jack: *That's all it takes, eh? Coulda told me sooner. All right, all right. I'll hit you up later when I've had some kip.*

October 28

11:30 p.m.

Will: *How long are you sleeping for? One hundred years?*

November 1

02:30 p.m.

Jack: *Don't get your knickers in a twist, mate. Okay, Okay, here's the thing. You know I've been mixing my own tracks this year? Well, XS have offered me an album deal… for my own stuff, not just mixing up a compilation. Awesome, right? BUT, I hate their graphics, so I put a clause in my contract that I'd source my own artwork… CD sleeves, web graphics, promo shit. SO, I need a graphic designer to come on board and help me out….*

Do you see where I'm going with this?

03:45 p.m.

Will: *I think so, but be clear.*

04:23 p.m.

Jack: *Don't be a twat. Okay, how's this: WILL YOU DESIGN MY ALBUM COVER PRETTY PLEASE WILL I'LL LOVE YOU FOREVER. Clear enough?*

04:45 p.m.

Will: *Would've been better with some punctuation, but yeah, I'll give it a go. Maybe I can use it in my finals next year. Do you have something in mind?*

05:10 p.m.

Jack: *Nah, I trust you. You know what I like. I've got a spec brief from XS, though. I'll post it to you. And don't rush. They want to see something by January 31, so you have plenty of time.*

05:30 p.m.

Will: *Okay. I'll get something together for you by Christmas then. Are you coming home anytime in December?*

06:04 p.m.

Jack: *I'm not booking any gigs Christmas through New Year. My mum said she'd disown me if I didn't spend a week at home with her. So, yeah… show me what you got then and we'll figure it out. Gotta run, I'm playing at G-Fest tonight. Love ya*

December 2003

Towcester. England.

WILL BIT down on his bottom lip as he fiddled with the

settings on the gradient tool. He was working on a graphic style for Jack's album sleeve and he'd reached a crucial part. A wrong move now would mean he'd have to start over… again, and he was running out of time for fuckups.

He scrutinized the screen. The effect he'd created was metallic and grungy, perfect for the text he planned to use for Jack's DJ alias, or so he hoped. He'd designed dozens of CD sleeves over the years, for school and for his own amusement, but this was the first time he'd been paid for his work, and Jack's record company was paying him a *lot*, enough to pay six months of rent up front, easing the burden of crippling student debt.

At least, they would if Will ever finished the projects *and* they liked them. Two things that still felt totally fucking impossible.

And, of course, Jack had to like it too, which was why, three hours after arriving home, Will sat at his dad's kitchen table, scrabbling together his project folder, instead of dashing next door to see Jack for the first time in six months.

It *had* to be perfect, dammit.

Will got lost in his work and time got away from him. The sound of his dad's key in the door took him by surprise a little while later. He checked the time: 7:00 p.m. Oops. He saved his work and put the kettle on. Ned Barter was a creature of habit and liked a cup of strong instant coffee the moment he walked through the door. Will didn't usually bother to wait on him, but it was Christmas Eve, and his father had been working for the last fourteen hours.

Will set the mug on the table just as his father filled the kitchen doorway.

"You're back, then," Ned said.

"Looks that way." Will had finished uni for the Christmas holidays two weeks ago, but while his housemates had all gone home, he'd stayed in Leeds, working in a call center to make extra cash.

Ned swiped his mug. "Good trip down?"

"On the coach? Yeah, it was bloody lovely, squashed up against some old bloke who hadn't washed for a week."

"No need for lip, lad." Ned grunted and took a swig of his coffee. "I'm going to have a shower. What are you doing later? Want to head down the Lion? I'll get the first round."

The only plans Will had involved Jack, but it had been a while since Ned had offered to buy him a drink. Ned was at peace with Will's sexuality, but there was still a part of him that pegged Will too gay for manly things like father-son pub time.

Will shut his laptop down while Ned stomped off to wash away a day of warehouse grime. He listened to Ned sing Fleetwood Mac, then darted out of the back door to catch a few minutes with Jack before Ned came back.

He knocked on the Lawsons' front door. It took a while, but eventually, Jack's younger sister cracked it open an inch.

Will smiled. "Hey, Laurie. Is Jack there?"

Laurie peered at him from behind her fringe, face impassive. She was twelve and not quite at the sullen scowling stage of puberty. "Jack's in Ibiza."

"I thought he got back on Monday?"

"He did, but he left again yesterday."

Will felt like he'd been punched in the gut. "He left?"

Laurie shrugged. "Last night. Mum's cross because he left his presents behind."

There wasn't much else to say. Will drifted home, his mind in bits. Jack's e-mails had become sporadic again over the past few weeks, but Will had assumed he was working a lot to make up for his Christmas break. Will kicked the back door shut. His stomach churned. Why would Jack change his plans? And why the fuck wouldn't he tell Will? Sacking him off was one thing, Will could handle that, but the silence? Yeah. That fucking hurt.

Ned appeared in the kitchen, dressed in jeans that could've done with another turn in the washing machine. "What's up with you? Look like you've seen a ghost."

Will huffed and retrieved the keys from the backdoor. "Nothing. Are you ready?"

They sloped into town and took up residence at the bar in the local pub. Ned seemed pretty much molded to the stool by the dartboard, and Will wondered how often he came down here now Will was away for most of the year. They'd lived in the same house for eighteen years, and there were days when they exchanged only grunts, but Will knew Ned looked into his room every night—or morning, depending on when he came home from work—and checked he was safe, even if he was sharing his bed with Jack.

Jack. Will's spirits sank again. Until he'd knocked on Jack's door, he hadn't realized how much he'd invested in spending Christmas with Jack. *Pathetic much*?

Ned bought another couple of pints. He slid one to Will. "All right. I've had enough of the sulking. Spit it out, lad. Something going tits up in Leeds?"

"Leeds is fine, Dad. You'd know that if you ever came up to see me."

"And when do you expect me to do that, eh? In between night shifts? Besides, I reckoned you'd want to forge your own way up there, away from your old dad."

Will traced the rim of his frothy glass with his fingertip. "My own way? You think I didn't live my own life down here?"

Ned shrugged. "I didn't give you much choice. With your ma gone, I've had to trust you to look after yourself, but I know there's not much around here for, um, blokes like you."

Will rolled his eyes. "Fuck's sake, Dad. Just call me gay. It's not catching."

Ned bristled. "Hey, now. Don't give me grief about that. I do my best. Your granddad would've had me by the balls if I'd come home and told him I was a poof."

"*Dad.*" Will glanced around, but no one was looking their way. Besides, everyone knew Will was gay. "No one says poof anymore. It's fucking offensive."

"I know." Ned eyed Will. "That's why I only say it when I'm talking about your granddad. You think I didn't give myself a crash course in the lingo when you first attached yourself to that boy next door?"

"What? Jack? Piss off, Dad. You know he's not gay."

Ned caught the barmaid's attention and bought a scotch. "Whatever. I reckon I knew which way you swung before you did, so I got meself down the library and read some books. Probably all outdated now, but I think I did all right, so stop giving me stick."

Will watched Ned nurse his scotch, swirling the amber liquid in the glass until it became a glowing prism in the light of the pub's open log fire. Books? Ned? Really? "You never told me that."

"Never saw the need. You seemed to have it all sorted, but you look depressed today. If Leeds is fine, what's put that scowl on your face? Trouble in your, er, love life? What happened to that Ewan boy you brought back in the summer?"

Will sighed. "Evan, Dad. His name was Evan, and I know you didn't like him, so don't pretend any different."

Ned had the grace to nod. "I'm never going to like a bloke who walks into my house and tells me it ain't worth insuring."

"That's not what he meant," Will protested, though he knew there was little point. He and Evan had parted ways amicably after Will had come to realize the only place their personalities didn't clash was in bed—and even then it felt tenuous—but he didn't miss him. Not in the slightest. Never gave him a thought.

No, because you only think of Jack, don't you? Awake. Asleep. In bed with someone else. He's always on your mind.

Evan was a dick in many ways, but he'd been right about that.

With considerable effort, Will pulled his thoughts from Jack and made an attempt to spend a cheery Christmas Eve with his dad. And it worked, for a while. Watching Ned work the dartboard like a pro and flirt with the barmaid was a sight for sore eyes, and Will realized how much he'd missed his dad's unobtrusive company.

It didn't last, though. Around eleven, the barmaid rang the bell for last orders and Will and Ned headed home.

Will walked with his head down, hiding from the drizzle and gloom of the damp December night, his mind a mile ahead of him, staring into the empty bedroom at the back of Jack's house. It had been more than a year since Will had slept with Jack—in any context—but the thought of heading home to his own empty childhood bed felt like the worst thing in the world. And what about the album sleeve? Was Jack's absence deliberate? Was he trying to tell Will something? Perhaps the record company had come to their senses and refused to pay an untried student a small fortune to do a job a professional could do much better.

Ned slung his arm around Will's shoulders. "Want a fag?"

"Gave up, Dad."

"Good for you." Ned shook out his cigarettes and lit up. "Never liked you smoking. Reminded me of all the shit I'd done wrong."

"Then you should've stopped me." Will kicked at an empty crisp packet. "I probably only did it to get your attention."

"That right?"

Will shrugged. "Maybe. Jack's dad grounded him for a week when he caught us. You never said a bloody word."

"Didn't see the point. You knew it was wrong. What good would grounding you do? And I was never around to keep you in anyway."

Ned had a point, and sniping at him for his well-meant wisdom didn't make Will feel any better. They turned onto their street. Will pulled the back door keys from his pocket. "You're right. I'm sorry…."

He caught sight of a huddled figure on the doorstep. For a

moment he thought it was Jack. His heart leaped. Then the figure rose and pushed his hood back, and Will realized it was George, Jack's younger brother. "George? You all right, mate—"

"Piss off. I see you still get your nice fucking family Christmas."

"Eh?" Will frowned, shocked at the venom in George's tone. "Something wrong?"

George scowled. He was younger than Jack by three years and as highly strung as Jack was laid-back. "You made Jack gay."

"Excuse me?"

George took a few steps forward and thrust something into Will's hands. "You made him a faggot. Look. What do you think my dad said when this landed on our doorstep yesterday morning?"

In Will's peripheral vision, he saw Ned flank him, put his shoulder between him and George, ready to intervene if George came any closer. Will looked down at the crumpled magazine. It was a copy of *Mixmag*, the publication Jack had forbidden Will to buy after they'd put his music in a box he didn't like. "What the fuck?"

"Open it." George spat on the ground. "Page thirteen. I'm guessing the bloke Jack's snogging ain't you, but I bet you gave him the bloody idea. Fucking faggot."

"Oi. We'll have none of that." Ned stepped in front of Will, blocking George from Will's view.

But there was no need. Will found the right page in the magazine, and his world narrowed to the tiny, blurred photograph that turned the world upside down.

It was Jack, laid out on one of those stupid bloody couches in Pacha, locked in an embrace with… a motherfucking man.

Beneath the image was some shit about Jack confirming the rumors he swung both ways. Will stared at the words, but couldn't take them in. What fucking rumors? Jack was straight. He'd always been straight.

Hadn't he?

Will dropped the magazine. It fell in a puddle by the drain. "That isn't me. I haven't seen Jack since July, so I don't know what the fuck you're talking about."

He started to walk on, past George and Ned and that damn bloody magazine, but George stopped him with a bitter laugh.

"I know it's not you, but you're the only gay boy Jack knows, and my dad says you fucking brainwashed him. Said he went to Ibiza to get away from you, but it was too late."

Like your manwhore dickhead dad would ever know why Jack went to Ibiza. Like he ever knew anything but which bird he was screwing next. The retort was on the tip of Will's tongue, but he bit it back. Whatever was going on, George was old enough to figure his father's shortcomings for himself.

Will closed his eyes briefly. "Listen, I don't have a clue who your brother is doing what with, or why. If you want to know, you should probably ask him."

Will walked into the house and let the door slam shut behind him. He walked to the fridge. Opened it. Shut it. Opened it again and stared at the bare shelves. They were spending Christmas Day with Ned's sister so there'd been no need to stock up on anything more than beer and milk.

The back door opened and shut. Ned. Will let the fridge close, killing its glimmer of light, but he didn't turn around until he felt Ned's hand on his shoulder.

"Sit down, lad. I'll put the kettle on."

Will sat. Ned was the kind of bloke you didn't ignore, even when that stupid bloody magazine, wet from the puddle, was laid out on the kitchen table. Ned plonked down two mugs of tea. He picked up the magazine. Flipped it over so the offending photo was all Will could see.

"George said he gets this so he can follow Jack, know where he's playing and whatnot. Reckons Jack calls home less than you do."

Neither statement surprised Will. George had always idolized Jack. What brother wouldn't? Strong, handsome, sporty, and musical, Jack had it all. And Jack never called home because he didn't want to hear his mum witter about how hard his dad was working on his millionth business trip of the month.

Will sighed. "Jack's been really busy lately, but I didn't know anything about this, I swear."

"I believe you," Ned said. "Even if I didn't, your face don't lie. Never could. Feel sorry for that boy out there, though. He reckons Jack and his old man had words last night. Woke up this morning and Jack was gone. Sounds rough. Think George was more excited 'bout having his big brother home for Christmas than he wanted to let on."

Will drew his tea close, wrapped his hands around the mug, and tried to let the warmth back into his heart. He felt bad for Jack, George, and the rest of their family. If Jack was hiding something, none of them deserved for it to come out this way, but beneath that, anger crept through Will like cold, sludgy poison that swallowed every moment of joy and happiness he'd ever spent with Jack.

Jack had kissed a man who wasn't Will, and no amount of tea and sympathy would ever ease the pain in Will's chest.

CHAPTER SIX

DECEMBER 26
 10:34 a.m.
 Will: *Did you make it back okay?*

December 27
 11:15 p.m.
 Will: *Jack? You there? Come on, mate. Don't blank me now. My dad bought me a phone for Christmas. The number is at the top of my e-mail account page. Call me. Or send me one of those text things.*

December 28
 07:05 a.*m.*
 Will: *JACK....*

2004
 January 1
 09:47 a.m.
 Jack: *Sorry, mate. Haven't turned the computer on for a week.*

Dodging the hate mail from my dad. Sorry I missed you at Christmas. Things got a bit lairy. How are you?

09:59 a.m.

Will: *That's it? Are you taking the piss? What the fuck happened?*

January 2

08:15 a.m.

Jack: *You know what happed. George told your dad.*

08:23 a.m.

Will: *I want you to tell me.*

January 4

08:34 a.m.

Jack: *Tell you what? That I got off with a bloke? Chill your beans, mate. It wasn't a big deal. I was trashed, and it felt right at the time. Can't believe the cameras caught me. They never take pictures in that room.*

08:56 a.m.

Will: *That's it? Fuck's sake, Jack.*

January 6

09:05 a.m.

Jack: *What?*

January 9

11:10 p.m.
Jack: *Helloooo? Answer your phone.*

January 12
08:48 a.m.
Jack: *I know you're not dead. My mum saw your dad in Tesco.*

January 18
09:55 a.m.
Jack: *Whatever.*

January 31
11:58 p.m.
Will: *I finished the XS project. The file is attached.*

February 1
08:48 a.m.
Jack: *Does this mean you're talking to me again?*

February 3
08:34 a.m.
Jack: *Obviously not….*

July 2004
Leeds. England.

WILL SPUN his office chair in a lazy circle. Working in a call center was a crock of shite, especially one servicing a gas company at this time of year. Whose central heating broke down in July? And who cared? Not Will—he just needed the

63

money, which was why he was spending his summer break locked inside a dingy office.

A phone rang. Will grabbed his desk to break the spin of his chair. He turned his headset on. Nothing happened. It took him a moment to realize the ringing was coming from his own phone.

He dug the phone out of his bag. *Private number* flashed up on the tiny screen. He pressed the call button, but he already knew what he'd hear—nothing. He'd had many calls like that in recent weeks, spooky and silent. Sometimes he felt convinced he could hear someone breathing, but other times he knew it more likely an automated call center had his number jammed in a glitch in their database. He knew all too well how often that happened, and this time, there was no sound on the line, nothing at all, not even the whir of a computer-controlled communication system.

Will killed the call and tossed the phone on his desk. He was alone in the office, handling the dull as dust six-till-twelve graveyard shift on his own, like he did most Thursday nights at this time of year. So far, he'd handled three calls, and one of those had been an order for chicken chow mein. He was bored, seriously fucking bored, so he turned to his favorite source of distraction—pissing about on his graphics software.

He shoved a disc into the drive on his desk. The office computers were far better than the computer he had at home, and he often took advantage of his lonely evening shifts to get his uni work done. He loaded his project folder and opened the image he had in mind to develop over the next year. It was a multilayered piece already, but he'd seen a robot poster he fancied a crack at. He opened his sci-fi folder and scrolled through his saved images. An unnamed file caught his eye. He clicked on it and realized his mistake too late to stop Jack's album cover filling the screen.

Will sat back in his chair and scowled at the screen. The media pack he'd produced for Jack was some of his best work

—too good to delete—which meant every time he saw it he found himself looking through the futuristic, electrostyle masterpiece and instead seeing the photograph of Jack snogging a bloke. The stupid bloody photograph that haunted Will's dreams, taunted him from beyond his subconscious like it was something that mattered, rather than the daft teenaged angst Will had come to accept it actually was.

Most days, at least. It had taken him a while to become so pragmatic.

Will closed Jack's file and opened another, where he'd saved the regular e-mails he and Jack had exchanged up until last Christmas. He clicked through them, lingering on Jack's, checking for any sign he'd missed that Jack had been showing an interest in blokes, but he found nothing, like every other time he'd repeated the exercise, which was more often than he cared to admit. He'd got over his anger with Jack—after all, it wasn't as though Jack owed him anything after a quick bunk-up two years ago—but communication between them had slowed in recent months, and Will no longer let himself sit up at night, waiting on something that made his bones itch.

Fuck that shit. Will checked the date. It was July 30 and he hadn't spoken with Jack in more than a month. Healthy distance, that's what Suki called it the long nights Will had sat up chewing her ear off, and eventually he'd come to realize she was right. He'd seen nothing but Jack for far too long, and it was time for a change.

Shame Will missed him so much it hurt.

———

A FEW weeks later, Will shut down his office computer after a tedious Friday evening at the call center, gathered his things, and headed for the door. He caught a bus home to an empty house and took a shower. Ten hours trapped in the airless call center had made him smell like arse.

He emerged from the bathroom to eight missed calls from a Reading number. Curious, he dropped some money into the payphone in the hallway and called it back. It rang out a few times. Will wasn't sure what made him try again, but on the third go a woman answered.

"HMV, Reading. Can I help?"

"Erm." Will floundered. HMV? What the fuck? "I got some missed calls from you, at least I think I did. I might have dialed back the wrong number."

"Your name's not Will Barter by any chance, is it?"

"How did you know?"

The woman laughed. "Because there's a note taped to the phone telling me to listen out for your call. Hang on a moment, I'll go and get him."

Him? The line switched to some awful lift music while Will drummed his fingers on the wall. The woman was gone for so long his money ran out. He was scrabbling about for change when the phone rang again.

Will grabbed it, breathless. "Hello?"

"Will? That you?"

Jack. Fuck. Will hadn't heard his voice for more than a year. "Er, yeah. It's me. Jack? It is you, right? What the fuck are you doing in Reading?"

"Work." There was a rustling at Jack's end, then quiet, like he'd shut a door on a room… or a shop, full of people. "A few of us came over to launch an album for XS and play some festivals. I've been ringing your phone for weeks. I've got a set at Reading tonight, then I was thinking of playing Leeds tomorrow, if you'll come with me?"

"You're in Leeds?" Will swallowed hard. With Jack far away in Ibiza, it had been all too easy to pretend he didn't exist. That Will wasn't breaking his heart over something that had never existed in the first place.

Jack chuckled. "Not yet. I'm in Reading now, but there's a gig going at Leeds and no one at XS wants it. I said I might plug the gap, but I don't want to party on your turf without you. What do you say? Up for a mash-up?"

"Um…." Will was lost for words. He'd pretty much resigned himself to never seeing Jack on UK soil ever again, though the explanation for his sudden reappearance explained the strange silent phone calls.

"I can get you in for free, if you're worried about money. I can meet you at the gate." Jack paused. Will could almost see him wrapping his fringe around his index finger, chewing on his bottom lip. "You're still fucked off with me about Christmas, aren't you?"

"It's not that." Will sat down amongst the mess of junk mail and take-away menus. "I'm still in Leeds because I'm working, remember? I'll have to change my shifts around."

"Do you think you can?"

Will shrugged before he remembered Jack couldn't see him. "I can try. Does your mobile work in the UK? I can call you later if I figure it out."

"Yeah, it works." Jack sounded deflated. "I might not hear it, though, if I'm on stage. Leave me a message. I'll call you back."

There wasn't much left to say. Jack hung up and left Will sitting in the hallway of his deserted student house, pondering what the fuck to do next.

WILL GRIPPED the phone so hard it creaked, like it would surely snap. "I'm not going. I can't go, can I? It's a stupid fucking idea, isn't it?"

Suki laughed, though it sounded kind rather than mocking. "I don't know, babe. You haven't seen him since last summer. Maybe you should go, clear the air a bit. You haven't talked about, well, anything with him, have you? You've been blanking him since that magazine thing. Never gave him a chance to explain."

"He didn't *want* to explain." Will scowled at a piece of chewing gum stuck to the ground. Kicked it. "And it doesn't bloody matter anymore, anyway. I'm over that shit."

"Yeah? So what's the problem? If you're sound with it, go to the festival and party with your oldest friend."

Put like that and combined with Will's unwillingness to admit how screwed up his feelings for Jack still were, there wasn't much Will could say. Besides, he was outside the festival ground, hiding in a phone box, just a few feet from where he'd agreed to meet Jack. There was no going back now, and his panicked call to Suki's parents' house in Staines had done nothing to ease the sickening churn in his belly.

Will garbled a good-bye to Suki and rang off. He lingered a moment longer in the phone box, like he could pocket the claustrophobic sanctuary and take it with him. A sense of the ridiculous crept over him. *Man up, you daft twat.*

He forced himself out of the phone box. The heat of a rare scorching day took him back to the previous summer in Ibiza, when he'd stepped off the plane and near enough run straight into Jack's arms—platonically, of course. It wouldn't be like that this time, if Will ever found the balls to cross the road. He didn't know much, but of that he was certain. Something undefined had changed between them, and Will wasn't sure he could face it.

He crossed the road anyway and scanned the busy entrance, searching among the stewards and students passing out leaflets for any sign of Jack. Not that he knew what he was looking for. So much had changed; Jack could've dyed his hair purple for all Will knew.

A warm hand clamped down on Will's shoulder. Jack. It had to be, no one else could light Will on fire by touch alone, and sure enough, he turned and found himself face to face with all sandy-haired six foot of Jack bloody Lawson.

Jack offered a tentative grin and pulled Will in a man hug they'd shared a thousand times over. "All right, mate?"

Will mumbled into Jack's shoulder.

Jack pulled away. "What's that?"

"Sorry I'm late."

"Who cares?" Jack's smile widened enough for Will to believe him. "You're here now, ain't ya? Where's your bag? You can dump it in the van if you want."

"I didn't bring a bag. I live twenty minutes away."

"Oh. Okay. Do you want to come and see some new DJs play, then? I've found this wicked Geordie kid I want you to hear. Are you coming in or what?"

Despite the blunt, playful question, Jack seemed nervous. He looked just the same as Will remembered him, but there were shadows under his eyes and his hands twitched. Will wondered if Jack had succumbed to the drug culture around him in Ibiza. Wondered if the heavy air between them was chemically manufactured and not his own fault after all.

But the fantasy didn't last long. Will stared at Jack for a long moment and realized that maybe Jack wasn't the problem. Perhaps it was Will, and perhaps it always had been. So much hung between them, both imagined and real, but as the noise of the festival reached Will—the music, the crowds—and the sun warmed his face, he realized he didn't care. He'd been Jack's friend for as long as he could remember, and this was what they did—partied outdoors around campfires, raving to dirty beats… this *was* them. Bottom line: there was no "or what."

"I'm coming in."

Jack laughed like he'd been set free. He grabbed Will's arm and fixed an all-access pass he produced from nowhere around Will's wrist. Then he hustled Will through a security-manned gap in the fence, and Will let himself be carried away by the magic of just being with Jack, the magic he'd been without for so long he'd forgotten how good it felt.

They found a beer tent and loaded up on plastic cups of nasty lager; then Jack led the way to the intro stage. The new DJs were good, and as the music took over Will's soul, he felt the last strains of tension seep out of him. He'd always loved festivals—the freedom, the spirit—and combined with Jack glued to his side, talking his ear off, there was nothing else in the world.

At least nothing that seemed to matter.

They drank their way through the heady summer crowds. Jack was recognized from time to time, but when they got to the VIP area beside the stage Jack was going to play on later that night, the attention faded. To Will, it felt like *everyone* lounging around the campfire was someone he'd seen on the front of a magazine.

Jack got them more drinks, nodded to a few people he knew, then steered Will to a quietish corner where they could see the stage.

Will sat on the grass and leaned back on his hands, looking out over the crowds. "So this is how superstars do festivals? No portaloos and shithole tents for you, eh?"

"Yep. They call it glamping… glamorous camping, get it?" Jack chuckled, though it sounded hollow. "To be honest, mate, I don't like it much. Feels like I'm missing all the fun, but work's work, you know? This is the first time I've been so early to a gig in ages."

Will snorted. "You're never early to anything."

"That's not true." Jack stared at Will a moment, like he was waiting for Will to fill in the punchline. "Um, anyway. How's things with you? I saw your old man yesterday. He said you aced your end of year exams."

"You saw my dad? Where? Back home? What were you doing there?"

"What do you think?" Jack lit a cigarette. "My mum was threatening to get on a plane. Figured I needed to show my face and head her off."

"What about your dad? I mean, wasn't that weird after what happened at Christmas?"

Jack blew out a lungful of smoke. "He wasn't there. He's moved in with his secretary."

Fuck. Will didn't know what to say. "Is your mum okay? What about George and Laurie?"

"That's a lot of questions for someone who's been blanking me for six months." Jack lay back on the sun-scorched grass and closed his eyes. "George is like me. Doesn't care. Laurie's upset, though. She doesn't want to sleep over at Dad's new place. She's too young to realize *he* probably won't want that either."

Jack's tone was bleak. Will reached out, his hand hovering over Jack's bare arm, itching to comfort his best friend, but after a protracted pause, he let his hand drop. Being with Jack felt good, almost normal, but touching him? Nah, Will wasn't ready for that. "When did your dad leave?"

"A few weeks ago, but it's been on the cards for a while. I think he was going to go at Christmas, but I fucked up his plans."

It was the first time either of them had alluded to *that* photo since their terse e-mail exchange back in January. Will considered letting it go, ignoring the awkward silence and pretending it had never happened at all, but the months of tension hung over him like a cloud, and in that moment, he'd had enough.

Will sat up. The sudden movement roused Jack. He rolled over and stubbed out his smoke. But he said nothing. Still. After all this time.

"Who was he?"

"Who?"

"The bloke in the photo."

Jack shook his head. "Fuck, no. You don't get to do that. Don't ignore me for months and then play it like you give a shit."

Will blinked. "Give a shit? What's that supposed to mean?"

"What do you think? That you can just—" Jack shoved a hand into his hair and squeezed his eyes shut. He opened them again with a heavy sigh. "Just forget about it, okay? I fucked up and dropped some pills. I was rushing my nuts off and thinking of the best kiss I'd ever had. I would've got off with anyone that night just to find it."

Will took a breath, but he was cut off by someone calling Jack's name. A big, bearded bloke who turned out to be Ray, Jack's manager. Jack was due on stage in a few hours and he had shit to do.

Jack came and went for a while after that, busy with setup and stage prep. Will watched him work, oddly fascinated. How had he missed Jack growing up and becoming a man who made decisions about lighting and speaker feeds? What happened to the boy who cared for nothing but beats? Will found himself mourning the precocious teenager who'd rocked all-night raves armed with just a vague set list and a bucketload of balls.

Jack went on stage at midnight to a capacity crowd. He'd tried to convince Will to sit in the booth, but Will had shaken his head and slipped away into the arena, eager to see Jack the way everyone else did: from the ground. He found a space in the center of the crazy crowd, and like he'd been doing all damn day, he watched. From time to time, it crossed his mind that he looked pretty strange, standing stock-still in the middle of a buzzing festival crowd, gaze fixed on the dude half-hidden by the towering stacks of sound equipment around him, but he didn't much care. Instead he compared the show to the one he'd seen in Ibiza and decided Jack looked much happier playing in the open air, away from the stifling claustrophobia of the Ibizan club. Jack wasn't much of a showman, preferring to let the music do the talking. In Ibiza he hadn't so much as glanced at the crowd, but it felt different here. *Jack* felt different. His stance, concentrated frown and… wait. *Why's he grinning like an idiot?* Though Will could hardly see Jack, he'd recognize his smile from the ends of the earth. Jack was laughing, and when he played his last track, Will knew why.

Cheeky bastard….

Will burst out laughing and felt an instant pull to be by Jack's side. The kind of pull that overrode the lingering disquiet between them. He pushed his way through the crowd and back to the VIP barrier. It took a while. He flashed his pass and reached the stage exit as Jack was jumping down the steps, wired and flushed, eyes bright, hair sticking up in every direction.

Jack jumped on Will and lifted him from the ground. "Did you hear it? Did you hear it?"

"Hear it?" Will let Jack spin him around until he felt so dizzy his laughter stuttered to a gargle in his throat. "Of course I heard it. The whole bloody world heard it. I can't believe you remixed a Craig David track. You hate his stuff."

Jack set Will down but held him in place with a stare that Will felt all over. "I know, but you played that song twenty times a day the summer it came out. Thought that garage shit might get you moshing."

Will laughed again, like he would never stop. Garage music was a long-running bone of contention between them. Will liked it. Jack didn't. At all. Refused to play it. Ever. "It didn't sound much like garage to me, but I fucking loved it. You should mix all his stuff as drum-and-bass."

"Fuck, no." Jack chuckled and finally seemed to notice how close they were standing. He released Will and stepped back. "I only did that for you, and I don't get to play much DnB these days. Ibiza's all about the trance."

Jack pulled a face that made him look about twelve. Will stared, transported back to a time when Jack *had* been twelve and that face had been Will's constant companion. It felt like another life, like they'd both been somebody else, but at the same time, it felt like yesterday.

"What are you staring at?" Jack said. "Have I got something on my face?"

"Eh?" Will shook himself. "Your set was amazing. I loved it. And look…." Will pulled Jack to the barriers so they could see the crowd. "Listen to that: they're still shouting your name."

Jack grinned. "We should go and party with them. I haven't been in a mosh for ages."

"Won't you get mobbed?"

"Nah. Hang on." Jack ducked into a nearby tent and emerged with a baseball cap. He jammed it on his head and tucked most of his hair inside. "See? Perfect disguise."

Will wasn't convinced, but he led the way to the barriers anyway. It was two o'clock in the morning and the call of the kicking festival was too strong to ignore.

They passed through the barriers and lost themselves in the sweaty mob. For a while they partied by the main stage Jack had played on, jumping around like idiots, laughing and chugging back plastic pints of cheap beer. Then they moved on, swept away by the crowd until they reached the jungle tent. The beats were lower in there, grittier, and they danced close together, stomping in the dirt and knocking shoulders with strangers.

Jack met Will's gaze and grinned, manic and high from the grimy rhythm of the music. He spun away and materialized behind Will, the heat of his body a hairsbreadth away.

"I've missed this."

Will closed his eyes and resisted the urge to lean back. "Me too."

He had to shout for Jack to hear him, and he didn't dare look to see Jack's face. Will was drunk... drunker than he'd been in a long time, and right here, right now, dancing with Jack under the stars, he felt like he'd been dropped in an alternate universe, a place where there was nothing but the scent of woodsmoke in the air and the sensation of Jack moving behind him.

Jack spun Will around. "I wanna tell you something."

"Yeah?" Will kept his eyes closed, still lost in the haze of music and Jack. "Something good?"

"I want to tell you about that kiss. What I was looking for when I snogged that bloke."

Will's eyes shot open. He made a grab for Jack's arm. Pulled him closer. Breathed him in, music forgotten. "Tell me."

Jack shrugged. "I was looking for you."

He danced away before Will could decide if he'd heard him right.

CHAPTER SEVEN

W ILL STUMBLED through his front door, dry-mouthed and bleary-eyed. He went straight to the kitchen and opened the fridge. "Do you want a Ribena?"

"Hmm?"

Will grabbed a carton and turned to find Jack casting his gaze around the shabby kitchen. "I warned you the place was a shithole."

"It's disgusting. I love it."

"Yeah, right." Will rolled his eyes. He wasn't quite sure how he'd ended up bringing Jack home. He'd caught the first early bus across the city, and for some reason, Jack had come with him. Neither one of them had questioned it. Perhaps it was the booze. Or the weed. Will felt too trashed to care much.

He drained his juice carton and chucked it on the side. "Do you want to see my room? It's in the basement."

Jack shrugged. He looked dazed and tired from their long night of partying. "Might as well."

Will led the way down the steep stairs of the seven-bedroom Victorian house. It was a typical student building, bedrooms crammed onto every floor, but Will had the cellar to himself, and even his own miniscule bathroom. The only thing missing was windows, save a tiny air vent he could just about squeeze through in case of a fire.

"So this is it, eh?" Jack paced the small room and stopped by Will's computer. "This is where the magic happens?"

"Magic? Don't know about that, but, yeah. This is where I sleep."

Jack made a noise that sounded like a grunt to Will's ringing ears. He sat on Will's bed. "It's dark in here. Must be a good place to hide."

"Not really. I live with a bunch of birds. I can't hide anywhere. I can't have a shower without one of them sitting on the bog, chewing my ear off."

Jack chuckled and lay back on Will's bed. He looked half-asleep, which made Will wonder if he should offer him a place to kip for the day.

Yeah, 'cause that won't make this weirder.

Will drifted to the bed and sat on the very edge, keeping his distance from Jack's long legs. "Where are you supposed to be right now? Will your manager wonder where you've gone?"

"Not likely. As long as I make the airport by noon tomorrow, no one gives a fuck where I am."

Will couldn't tell if Jack's flat tone meant anything. "Fair enough. So, uh, are you gonna stay here, then?"

"That okay?" Jack cracked an eye open. "I can go and find my hotel room if you want."

"No! Uh, no. Don't do that." Will pursed his lips and wished he could slap his hand over his mouth without making himself look more of a twat. "It's fine. You can sleep in here. I'll take Suki's room upstairs. She left her duvet behind."

Jack looked like he wanted to say something, but he didn't. He kicked his shoes off and rolled over, facing Will, eyes closed. "Feels surreal being here with you. I'm scared to go to sleep."

"Yeah, looks that way."

Jack didn't reply, and though they'd been separated for far too long, Will remembered him well enough to know it was the last thing Jack would say for a while. He'd always been the same: talking Will's ear off one minute, dead asleep the next. Not like Will, who could lie awake for hours, pondering and wondering. Musing. Ruminating.

Which was exactly what he found himself doing an hour after he'd draped a blanket over Jack and retreated to Suki's room in the attic. Away from Jack and the buzz of the festival, his mind was in bits. He'd spent months convincing himself that his feelings for Jack were nothing more than an unrequited crush on his childhood best friend, but now? Shit. Jack had said so many things in past twelve hours to undo all that. Too many to count.

I've missed you.

I think about you all the time.

This song reminds me of you.

I remember you.

I was looking for you.

What the fuck did it all mean?

Will had no idea, and he finally fell asleep, imagining what life would be like if his wildest dreams ever came true.

WILL WOKE to bright sunshine streaming through the sky light in Suki's attic bedroom. He groaned and rolled over, but there was no escape. Suki's room felt like a bloody greenhouse.

He sat up and rubbed his hands over his face. It felt like he'd just blinked, but he could tell by the vicious sun it was close to midday. He sniffed himself and wrinkled his nose— beer, sweat, and weed. Yep. He needed a shower.

He tiptoed to the third floor and stopped at the top of the stairs, listening. The house was silent and still, with no sign Jack had been up. Perhaps he'd gone. Will had taken his plans for "tomorrow" to mean Monday, but they'd been partying since Saturday afternoon. Perhaps he'd misunderstood and missed another good-bye.

Will made use of the girls' bathroom and washed away the mud and grime of his all-night rave. Then he crept downstairs to the basement in search of clean clothes. His bedroom was dark, too dark, and it took him a moment to see Jack had covered the tiny window with a T-shirt, and even longer to register a Jack-shaped lump hiding under the covers.

He stayed.

Will's heart skipped a beat. He stared a moment before he tiptoed to the canvas-covered shelving unit that held his clothes. He grabbed the first pair of tracksuit bottoms he found and glanced at the humped shape in the bed. Jack looked out for the count, so Will took a chance, dropped the towel, and scrambled into his clothes.

He started to leave, but halfway to the door something stopped him. An uneasy sensation in the pit of his stomach. A tingle on the back of his neck. Something felt off.

Will padded back to the bed and searched out Jack, who, at some point in the night… day, had burrowed under the covers and pulled a pillow over his head. Will found Jack's shoulder. Hard, tense muscles met his hand. Will frowned and shook Jack gently. "Jack? You all right, mate?"

Jack groaned. The sound was low and quiet, but unlike any noise Will had ever heard from him before.

Will leaned over the bed and pushed the covers and pillows away. Jack was shirtless and curled up in a ball, his face hidden by his arms. His hair was damp and he smelled clean, like he'd found his way to Will's bathroom at some point, but beyond the distraction of Jack's smooth skin, Will could tell something was seriously wrong. "Jack? What's up, mate? Talk to me."

Jack muttered something. Will leaned closer. "What's that? You've got a headache?"

"No…." Jack moved one of his arms a fraction. "Migraine."

Migraine. It took Will a moment to process; then he remembered one of his housemates, Lila, got migraines every month with her period. Spent two days curled up in her bed crying. One time it had been so bad Suki had called an ambulance. Shit. Since when did Jack get migraines?

Will sat on the edge of the bed and wrestled Jack's arms away from his face. Dazed, bloodshot eyes greeted him. Jack looked awful, pale and drawn, his body rigid with pain. "What do you need? What can I do?"

"Drugs. I've got some pills from the doctor in my wallet."

Will got up and searched out Jack's discarded jeans. He tried not to wonder what Jack was wearing on his bottom half and retrieved Jack's wallet. He found a foil strip of pills in one of the credit card slots. "How many do you need?"

"Two."

Will popped two pills out and fetched some water. Jack struggled to sit up. Will helped him and held the glass to his lips while he drank. After, it felt natural to wipe the spilled water from Jack's chin with the pad of his thumb.

Jack lay down again, his eyes clenched shut, in much the same position as before, hunched up in a ball, like he could squeeze the pain out of himself.

Will hovered, still holding Jack by his tensed-up shoulder. "Do you need anything else?"

Jack shifted. "No. Just…."

"What?" Will released Jack's shoulder from his death grip and rubbed his fingermarks away. "What do you need, mate?"

"Keep doing that thing with your fingers. It helps."

WILL SPENT an uncomfortable afternoon wedged between Jack and the wall. His back stiffened and his fingers ached, but he kept rubbing Jack's shoulders long after he felt the tension in Jack's muscles fade. Will didn't go back to sleep, but it was hours before Jack stirred. Will passed the time researching migraines and the name of Jack's pills on his laptop and, later, when he was sure Jack was fast asleep, watching footage of the festival on BBC2.

Jack woke around six. Will could tell straight away he felt better, though he remained pale and drawn.

Will removed his hand from Jack's shoulder and leaned back to give Jack space to move, space that Jack quickly filled by rolling face-first into Will's chest. Will braved a tentative arm around him. "Back with me, mate?"

Jack nodded and hummed his answer, and made no move to disentangle himself from Will's loose embrace. "What time is it?"

"Six. Hard to tell in here, isn't it? Window's so bloody small."

Jack grunted. "Was big enough to do my head in this morning."

Will glanced at the tiny window Jack had covered with his T-shirt and remembered what he'd read on the Net while Jack had been sleeping. "Was the light making your migraine worse?"

"How do you know about that?"

"You told me. Why do you think I'm in bed with you? You scared the crap out of me."

Jack blinked, like he wasn't entirely with it. "I don't remember that. I black out with them sometimes."

"Sometimes? This has happened before?" It seemed a stupid question, given the hard-core painkillers Jack had in his wallet, but Will needed to hear it from Jack.

"I had my first one six months ago. Since then, I've had about one a week, sometimes two. The doctors think it's the lights in the clubs, and the heat."

Will tightened his hold on Jack with little thought. "But we didn't go to a club. We were outside all night."

Jack shrugged. "I know. It's part of the reason I came. Figured I'd get away with it. Then they put some strobe lights on, remember? At the end? I felt kinda weird after that, but it didn't trigger the pain until we came back here."

"One a week? Fuck." Will shook his head and remembered Jack's dazed expression now, the way he'd shut down and passed out that morning. It was behavior he'd seen in Jack before, many times, but now he wondered if he'd missed something. "Are they always that bad?"

Jack huffed a soft puff of warm air into Will's chest. "I've had them much worse than that. One of my housemates found me passed out in the shower a few months ago. I don't remember it at all."

"That's not right, Jack." Will fought the urge to squeeze Jack tighter than he already was. "Isn't there anything you can do? Maybe you shouldn't play in the clubs anymore."

"It's not that easy. I'm locked into my XS contract for another two years. Even if they'd let me leave Ibiza, they'd only send me somewhere else just the same. I've tried to take more outdoor gigs and spend more time in the studio, but I'm fucked at the moment, and there's nothing I can do about it."

"What about your management?" Surely they didn't want Jack in such a mess after each gig? "What are they doing to help you?"

Jack shrugged. "Haven't told them. They'd probably release me from my contract, but I can't let that happen. If I fuck things up with them, I've got nothing."

Jack's misery was plain to see. It hurt Will's chest. He hugged Jack and absently kissed his hair, then he froze, mortified, but Jack didn't seem to notice. Perhaps he wasn't as recovered as he seemed.

That's right. He's ill and you're molesting him. Nice.

Will pulled his face from Jack's hair. "I did some reading while you were asleep. All the medical sites say you should take it easy. You don't have to be anywhere until tomorrow, do you?"

Jack shook his head.

"Good." Will rolled Jack gently onto his back and slid out of bed. "Stay there. I'll get you some tea."

Will left Jack and headed for the kitchen, searching for something... anything, to help Jack feel better. On his student budget that meant fish fingers, oven chips, and baked beans. He put the oven on, made tea, and took a mug back downstairs. Jack was in the bathroom. Will left his mug on the desk and returned to the kitchen.

Jack appeared just as Will was dumping their nursery supper on a couple of chipped plates. He looked like he'd showered again. "Did I throw up last night?"

"At the festival, or here?"

"Here." Jack started to scowl, then thought better of it. "I remember the festival."

Lucky him. Will had drunk so much the only thing he could recall with any clarity was the dizzying rush of dancing under the stars with Jack. "I don't know if you puked before I came down. Why? Do you feel sick now?"

Jack shrugged. "Not really. Bloody starving, too. How did you know I wanted a chip butty?"

"Because you're not as flash as you think you are." Will retrieved some clean cutlery from the draining board. When he looked back, Jack was sitting at the tiny kitchen table, watching, his expression unreadable.

They shared a quiet dinner. Jack inhaled his food, then nursed his second cup of tea. Will finished up and ditched the plates in a sink of hot water.

"Do you want me to wash up?"

Will glanced at Jack. "Nah, you're all right. I'll do it tomorrow. Give me something to do when you're gone. It's boring around here on my own."

"When do your mates get back?"

"Three weeks." Will came back to the table and leaned on his chair. He didn't feel like sitting down again.

"Must be weird being by yourself when you're used to all those birds running riot."

"It is." Will peered into Jack's mug. It was half-full. "Don't drink that yet. You need to take another dose of your pills."

"What are you? My mother?"

Will rolled his eyes. "What do you want to do tonight? I've got the first series of *Red Dwarf* on DVD. We can watch it on my computer if you're up to it."

Jack's expression brightened. *Red Dwarf* was his favorite TV program ever. "Sounds good to me."

They shuffled downstairs and settled on Will's bed again. Despite the balmy weekend, the heat and humidity had dropped during the day, and though it wasn't cold, the night was gray and bleak, and Will's basement room felt close and comforting. Like the real world and the strain of a blurred friendship didn't exist.

Jack sat with his back to the wall, but as the daylight faded, so did he. It wasn't long before he slumped down, leaning on Will, and dozed off.

———

WILL WOKE in the dark to a warm body curved around him, lips at his neck and a hard cock digging into his back. Will moaned and let his body respond before his brain caught up.

He rolled his hips back and tilted his neck to give those lazy, devilish lips better access. The heated mass behind him responded in earnest—tongue, teeth, and blunt nails. Fuck, those blunt nails. Will wriggled and groaned again, needing, craving more, until a sleep-thick, mumbled moan brought him to his senses.

Shit. Will jerked forward, his upper body flying off the bed. He saved himself with his hand, but his strangled curse was enough to wake Jack.

"Wha...? Will? What the fuck are you doing down there?"

"What do you think?" Will scrambled out of bed— somehow they'd ended up *in* the bloody thing, snuggled up like an old married couple—and put as much distance between him and Jack as possible in the tiny, dark room.

Jack squinted at him. "Did I kick you or something?"

"Or something." It came out as a growl, and the fiery depth of Will's anger surprised him. He'd shared a bed with Jack more times than he could remember, kissed him, touched him, fucked him, so why did this feel like the end of the fucking world?

Jack stretched and lay back, like a cat in the sun. Something inside Will snapped. He yanked the duvet off the bed and shoved Jack, hard. "Are you bloody serious? You're in my bed with your hands all over me and you're just gonna go back to sleep like nothing happened? Fuck you, Jack. I'm sick of this shit."

Jack blinked. "What—"

"Don't give me that crap. You sack me off at Christmas to bang some other bloke, all the while telling me how straight you are, then you turn up here, saying cryptic shit and messing with my head, and then you do this? Fuck you." Will took a breath and tried to quell his anger. Failed. "Listen, I don't know what the fuck's going on with you, but you don't get to walk in and out of my life like you give a shit when it's clear you don't. It's not fair, Jack. It's not fucking fair."

Will fled upstairs without waiting for Jack to respond, and when he woke from a fitful, restless sleep on the nasty Ikea couch, Jack was gone, leaving nothing but an empty packet of painkillers to show he'd been there at all.

CHAPTER EIGHT

SEPTEMBER 11

08:34 a.m.

Jack: *So… we haven't talked for ages and I don't really know what to say, but it's Monday morning and I'm drinking alone. Reckon I've got nothing to lose.*

Um, so… I'm sorry, I s'pose? It's taken me this long to figure it out, but I'm guessing I felt you up in my sleep, and you didn't like it. Shit. I really am fucking sorry, mate. Wish I could excuse it, or even explain it, but I can't. It's just… fuck, I don't know. Lately, I feel like I don't bloody know anything. And that's not even true, 'cause it's not a recent thing. I don't know how to say this, so I'm just going to say it: Having sex with you fucked with my head. And I've spent the last two years trying to figure out if it's the worst thing in the world or the best thing that ever happened to me.

I still don't know. I mean, I know it's not the worst thing in the world. How can it be when being with you makes me so happy? But I don't know what it means, for me, for you… I don't have a bloody clue. All I know is I came home to see you and ballsed it up, and for that, I really am sorry.

09: 38 a.m.

Will: *What the fuck??? You're telling me this now?*

11:34 a.m.

Will: *Okay, so I read your e-mail back when I wasn't half asleep, and I still don't get what you're trying to say.*

Jack, we've been mates our whole lives. I know things have been… weird since we left home, but I don't know what that means any more than you do. I've thought about it a lot… more than I want to admit, but all it boils down to is I kissed you and slept with you because I wanted to. You did because you felt sorry for me and you wanted a quick bang before you went to Ibiza.

It's taken me a while to figure that out. All this time I thought it didn't mean anything, but it does, even if it means something different for each of us. I'm gay. You're not. Yeah, you did grope me, but I liked it, so I'm not sure what I got the arse about.

Guess you're not the only one who's fucking confused.

10:45 p.m.

Jack: *Don't give me that. You know your own mind. Always have.*

September 12

01:48 a.m.

Will: *Do I? And does it matter? Jack, YOU'RE STRAIGHT.*

08:12 a.m.

Jack: *Am I?*

08:56 a.m.

Will: *Aren't you?*

· · ·

09:16 a.m.

Jack: *I don't know. I thought I was… always have, but then you… I've tried everything, Will. Nothing and no one feels like you.*

11:34 a.m.

Jack: *Please don't blank me. Not now.*

12:45 p.m.

Will: *I'm not. I was sleeping. And drunk. Still am. Maybe that's why this conversation doesn't feel weird. I wish we'd talked like this when you were here.*

12:57 p.m.

Jack: *Me too. We used to talk about everything. S'pose I fucked that up too.*

03:15 p.m.

Will: *No. Life just changed. But I miss you, Jack. Every day.*

10:38 p.m.

Will: *Now who's blanking who?*

September 13
   12:45 p.m.

Jack: *Sorry. Bad night. I miss you too, by the way. I wish I knew how to fix this.*

02:39 p.m.

Will: *Bad night? Migraine?*

09:45 p.m.

Jack: *Yeah. Can I ask you something? Fuck it. Gonna ask it anyway. What was it like when you first… got fucked by a bloke?*

September 23

02:23 a.m.

Will: *Why the hell are you asking me that?*

September 24

08:45 a.m.

Jack: *Stoned on migraine tablets. Seemed like a good idea at the time. But I do want to know. I remember fucking you. I dream about it sometimes. Not the fucking… your face at the end. I want to feel like that.*

09:15 a.m.

Will: *You're making my head spin and I have an assessment in half an hour I'm nowhere near fucking ready for, so I'm just going to say it…. Are you gay?*

02:45 p.m.

Will: *That didn't come out right. 'Cause it doesn't matter to me either way. Remember what you said to me? That providing I didn't want to bang your mum you'd be my mate whatever? It works both ways, Jack. The way I feel about you confuses me sometimes, especially when things… happen between us, but nothing matters more than being your mate.*

September 29

08:54 a.m.

Jack: *I used to think that too, until we did end up shagging. Then I woke up naked in your bed and nothing ever felt the same again. You should know, by the way, I'm pretty sure your dad walked in on us the next day. You were out of it, and I was kinda staring at you. I didn't notice him at the door till he was walking away.*

I counted the days after that until you left for Leeds. Then I had to leave for Ibiza and when I got there, I couldn't think straight. The girls, the money, the music. Something was missing, and I knew it was you. I figured we'd talk about it when you came to see me, but then I saw Evan waiting for you on the pavement and I realized for the first time that you weren't just mine.

Don't ask me why it took so long. Maybe it was Evan. He gave me this look and I knew he knew. I felt sick then, like the bottom of the world dropped out, and I didn't know why. Then you came to find me in the club. You fell asleep on me at Sunrise Rock and I knew that I was in deep fucking trouble.

Shit. I'm rambling again. Sorry, mate. It's just it all made sense when I saw you at the airport. That moment felt perfect, you know? I wish we could have that again.

08:23 p.m.

Will: *Hold that thought.*

September 30
   08:25 a.m.
   Jack: *Eh?*

07:45 p.m.
   Jack: *Will? Are you there?*

October 2004

Ibiza.

WILL SAT on the sun-warmed stone steps and shivered. He'd figured Ibiza would be balmy all year round, but as the daylight faded, Jack's doorstep felt as chilly as the English autumn he'd left behind.

His phone beeped, about to die. Stupidly, he'd dropped everything and got on a plane with just his wallet, passport, and a bag of clean clothes. He'd bought a toothbrush at the airport and batteries for his mini disc player, but his phone had drawn the short straw.

Idiot. Will shoved it in his pocket. He'd been sitting on the steps to Jack's apartment for hours, half dozing, half fretting. Jumping on a plane, still pissed up from a cheap wine-laden night in, moaning Suki's ear off, had seemed like a good idea at six o'clock in the morning—the only solution to weeks of e-mails that made no bloody sense. Jack's electronic confession had come in fits and starts, for both of them. Some days, Will couldn't open his e-mail for fear of what Jack would say next. Couldn't eat. Couldn't sleep. Then Jack took him back to the airport last summer. That heart-stopping moment when the world had narrowed to nothing but Jack… Will and Jack. Nothing but each other.

It's just it all made sense when I saw you at the airport. That moment felt perfect, you know? I wish we could have that again.

Three simple lines that had blown a gaping hole in Will's resolve. Since when had Jack become so bloody poetic?

Who knew? And even now, Will had little idea what he was doing, loitering outside Jack's building, waiting for him to come home. What the fuck was he going to do? Leap on Jack and confess undying love? Yeah, right. Because, really, what the hell had changed? Jack thought he might like cock… Will's cock in particular, and Will didn't know how he felt about that any more than Jack did.

Will retrieved his phone from his pocket. It still had half a bar of battery power, just enough to make the call he'd been meaning to make even before he'd lost his marbles and raided EasyJet's last minute flights.

Ned answered on the third ring. "Will? Where are you, son? Hang on, I'll call you back."

"Don't worry about it. I haven't got much battery anyway. Not in the pub or anything, are you? I want to ask you something."

Ned grunted. "Providing it's not dosh, we're good. That fancy computer of yours cleaned me out—"

"When were you going to tell me you saw me and Jack in bed together?"

"Eh? When?"

"A few summers ago. Before I moved to Leeds."

There was rustling at Ned's end, and the sound of a beer can popping. "Jack slept over every weekend, son. I saw you two crashed out in your bed all the time."

Will knew that. Of course he did. Ned had checked on him every day of his bloody life, but something about this felt off. "Don't bollocks me, Dad. Jack told me he saw you."

Silence. "He did, eh? Well, I s'pose I thought it wasn't my place. You'd already told me you were… gay, and you and Jack didn't seem any worse for it. No point me sticking my oar in."

"So you knew?" Frustration heated Will's blood. "All this bloody time, you knew about Jack and you didn't tell me?"

"Tell you what? Something going on?"

"I… I don't know." Will banged his head on his knees. He didn't quite have the balls to tell Ned he'd scarpered to Ibiza. "Things with Jack…."

"Ah, getting complicated? 'Bout bloody time. Surprised it's taken this long."

"What's that supposed to mean?"

Ned sighed, soft and gusty, like he'd been sighing Will's whole life, and Will heard it like a sonic boom. "Boy, you two have been wrapped up in each other since the day you met. Maybe it's time you thought about why—"

Will's phone died and took Ned's words of wisdom with it. The call also sapped the last of Will's energy. He pocketed the phone and kept his head on his knees. What the fuck was he even doing here? Ned was right. What kind of friendship was built around pity snogs and practice fucks? Jack was confused. He had to be. There was no—

"Will?"

———

JACK OPENED his front door with his flashy swipe card. He stood aside for Will to precede him. Will didn't move. Jack's appearance felt like a dream, and despite spending the last five hours slumped on his doorstep, Will felt lost, like he wasn't altogether sure where he was. Or how the fuck he'd got there.

"Will, come inside." Jack grabbed Will's arm and yanked him over the threshold.

Inside, they traipsed upstairs in silence. Jack pushed Will onto the sleek leather couch in the living room. He disappeared for a few minutes, then came back with tea and a packet of Bourbons.

Will stared at the biscuits. "You get those here?"

"It's Ibiza, mate, not Sierra Leone." Jack looked amused, though his red-rimmed eyes gave him away. "Eat some, please. It's all I've got in and you look half-dead."

Will could believe that. The last thing he recalled eating was a packet of Super Noodles straight out of the saucepan in Suki's bedroom, and he couldn't remember when he'd last slept. Shit, he hadn't slept properly in weeks.

He stuffed a few biscuits in his mouth. Jack watched him for a while, then edged closer and tucked Will's wayward hair behind his ears.

"Not that I'm not pleased to see you, but what are you doing here?"

Will glanced around. "Where are your flatmates?"

"Away. We're hardly ever here at the same time."

Jack's tone made Will look back at him. "So you're here by yourself?"

"Most of the time, yeah. Gets pretty lonely."

Something clicked in Will's brain. "You've said that to me before, at the festival."

Jack grinned, soft and faint. "Did I? Don't remember much about that."

Will sipped at his tea, then set it aside and let himself drift closer to Jack until he found himself leaning on Jack, his face buried in Jack's chest and Jack's arms around him like a warm, comforting cage.

Jack broke the deadlock first, though he didn't pull away. "Thought this would be easier if I could just see you, but it's not."

"Maybe I should go home so you can send me another bloody e-mail." Will stifled a Ned-style sigh and forced himself from Jack's loose embrace. "Sorry. That was twatish."

Jack let his arms drop. "Don't blame you. What is this? You here to tell me to go fuck myself?"

"What? No! It's not…." Will rubbed his temples. He'd had a stress headache all day. He couldn't imagine how Jack felt when his migraines hit. "Jack, I can't do this anymore, okay? I need you to tell me what the fuck's going on, and I need you to be really bloody clear what you mean."

Jack shifted. He sat back on his heels and bit his lip. "You said you'd be my friend whatever. Why does it matter how I feel about blokes?"

Will closed his eyes. "I don't give a shit how you feel about blokes. I care how you feel about *me*."

"Why?"

"Why do you think?"

Jack got up and put some much needed distance between them. "I don't know what to think. I meant everything I've ever said to you about… us, but I don't know how you feel. I never have."

"Are you taking the piss?"

Jack's expression darkened. "Me? Fuck you, Will. You think just because you're so bloody sure you're gay everything else just slots into place? That it's fucking obvious and you don't have to explain yourself ever again?"

Will was officially lost, and Jack's anger startled him. Jack was a passionate guy, but his temper was a slow burn, and Will hadn't seen him lose it in years. "Explain myself? What does that even mean?"

"Fuck's sake." Jack balled his hands into fists like he wanted to punch the wall. "I lost my virginity to you, and you walked away from me like it was nothing."

"What? Nothing? When did I ever say that? You said you wanted to fuck someone before you went to Ibiza. What was I supposed to think? That you were confessing your undying love?"

Jack shrugged. "Maybe I was and I didn't know it. But it doesn't matter, does it? And it didn't then, not to you. You packed up your shit and fucked off to Leeds without even saying good-bye."

"What the fuck? I'm not the one who didn't say good-bye, Jack. I came to your house, twice, but you weren't there. I even wrote you a letter. I gave it to your dad."

Jack stopped pacing. "My dad?"

"Yeah." Will stood, though to do what, he wasn't sure. He'd never asked Jack about that morning exchange with Derek Lawson. Never admitted how much it had hurt, not even to himself. "It was a Sunday morning, remember? My dad wanted to leave at 8:00 a.m. but I wouldn't get in the car until I'd seen you. But you weren't there. Your dad said you'd gone to footie, so I wrote you a note. He said he'd give it to you."

Jack was quiet for a long moment. It didn't take a genius to work out his grade-A tosser of a father had binned the letter and left him none the wiser. Will reckoned, given what had happened since at Christmas, he even knew why.

"What did the letter say?"

Will shrugged. "Nothing that would make this any better, but don't ever accuse me of not giving a shit, Jack, 'cause it's not true, and it's not fair. You can't play with my head because you think you might be gay, or bi, or whatever."

"Bi?"

"Jack, I saw you fucking some girl last time I was here, right here, in fact, on this bloody couch, so don't try and tell me you're not still messing about with birds."

"I haven't touched a girl since that night, and I didn't fuck her. I mean, I tried, but I couldn't finish. I took her back to the after-party and she went home with someone else."

"What about all those girls in the magazines?"

Jack shook his head. "Maybe at the start, but they recycle those pictures every week and put new captions over them. That one with the bloke? They've reprinted it six times this year already."

Oh. Will drifted closer to Jack with little conscious thought, backed him against the wall, and caged him with his arms. Jack was taller than Will, heavier and wider, but for the first time in years, Will felt in control of the craziness between them. "I'm going to ask you something, and I need you to tell me the truth, okay?"

"Ask me anything."

"Gay, straight, whatever, if I kissed you right now, how would you feel?"

Jack licked his lips. "Like I'd won the bloody lottery. It's been too long, Will. I don't know if I'm gay, and I don't give a fuck either way. I just know that doing this…." Jack gestured between them. "…only feels right with you. No one else makes me feel like this."

WILL PUSHED Jack down on his bed, on him before Jack could

take a breath. They kissed and rolled over, again and again, tangled in a frenzied race to undress each other.

Jack won… for the moment. He straddled Will's waist, pulled his T-shirt over his head, and stared, eyes gleaming in the dark of the room. He put his palms flat on Will's chest, unmoving, like he was trying to ground himself.

Will lay still, entranced by Jack's dark gaze. Then the heat of Jack's touch overran his control and all bets were off. Clothes became a distant memory, and before Will knew it, he was naked, hard, and covering Jack's body with his own, grinding them together, transfixed by Jack writhing and gasping beneath him.

He rose up on his hands and took in Jack's chiseled body. He'd lost weight in the last year. His boyish features were fading and leaving behind the hard, lean form of a man. A man Will could hardly believe was arching beneath him, begging… pleading for something more.

Will started to roll over. Jack stopped him.

"Can we do it the other way?"

"What?"

Jack gripped Will's shoulders, his chest heaving. "It's all I ever see when I think of this… of you. Please, Will. I want you to fuck me."

Will lay his hand over Jack's hammering heart. "Has there been… I mean, is it the first time?"

"Yeah." Heat colored Jack's cheeks. "I tried to once, with another guy, but I bottled it. I didn't want anyone else to touch me there."

A surge of possessive jealousy flooded Will's veins. He reclaimed his place covering Jack's body. "So what *did* you do with him, then?"

"Not much. Snogged him. Tossed him off, but I only did that because I felt bad about leading him on."

Will wanted to know more. Wanted to know everything, but more than that, he wanted to show Jack why he'd been right to say no to anyone that wasn't him. "Don't ever feel bad about not doing something that isn't right."

He swallowed Jack's reply with a kiss… a kiss that went on and on and became something deeper than they'd ever shared before. Will opened Jack with his fingers and tongue before Jack rolled onto his side and curled his leg to his chest.

"Wrap your arms around me."

Will smiled and moved to mold his body around Jack's, but he kept his hands free, one rolling a condom onto his cock and the other clutching Jack's shoulder. "In a sec. This bit might hurt. I'll be gentle."

Jack chuckled and leaned back into Will. He hooked his arm around Will's neck and tilted his face for a kiss. "I know it's going to hurt. I remember your face. You said it didn't, but I know it did."

"It stung a little." Will aligned them and pressed, careful at first, and then with more purpose, easing his way in. "But it wasn't my first time, so I knew it would get better."

"Better, eh? *Fuck*!" Jack hid his face in his arm, rigid.

Will rubbed his back. "Breathe. Don't fight it. You'll make it worse."

Jack panted out some harsh breaths. "When did you get so wise?"

"Shh. Just breathe."

Jack obeyed and Will slid inside him, slow and gentle, until he could go no further. Then he gave in to Jack's pleas and wrapped his arms tight around him, holding him like he was his most precious thing. He bit Jack's ear and nuzzled his neck, coaxing his face out of hiding. "I'm sorry I ever made you feel like this was nothing. It won't ever be nothing, Jack. Not for us."

Will fucked Jack like the world had stopped just for them. No deadlines, exams, or gigs waiting for them on the other side. He took Jack slow, rolling his hips, probing, pushing, searching for the cadence that slackened Jack's muscles and made him moan.

And moan Jack did, and he cursed and gasped and cried out until he fell forward and hid his face in a pillow. Will covered him and nudged his legs apart. Jack's trembling told him Jack was close to coming, but he doubted Jack knew it himself.

Will reached around Jack and found his cock, squeezed and stroked, coaxing an orgasm from Jack that even after all this time seemed to come from nowhere.

"Oh, God. Fuck. *Will*...." Jack lost it and exploded in Will's hand. A deep flush broke out over the skin Will could see, and his body tightened enough to push Will into a release that made his head spin.

Will groaned and fought the urge to slam into Jack and chase the heady pleasure. This wasn't about him. He pulled out. Jack hissed. Will tugged the condom off and eased Jack onto his back. "Back in a sec."

He padded to the bathroom, chucked the condom, and found a clean flannel under the sink. He soaked it with warm water and took it back to the bed. Jack was silent while Will cleaned up. He seemed spaced, and Will couldn't blame him. He'd been a dribbling wreck after that first time with Dave, and that hadn't felt anything like the heat between him and Jack.

"Washing basket's behind the door."

Will glanced down to find Jack staring at him. "I know. Think I can get it in from here?"

He chucked the flannel across the room without waiting for a response and watched it land on a teetering pile of dirty clothes. "Hope you haven't got a maid doing your washing. You okay?"

Jack hummed. "Yeah. I feel good... sore, but good. Hey, you know this wasn't like before, don't you? It's not an experiment, or some shit like that. I wanted this... still want it, with you."

Will smiled and pushed Jack's sweaty hair away from his face, still getting used to a naked Jack, in more ways than one.

"You know, I never let anyone fuck me after you. I've topped every shag I've had ever since."

"Does that include Evan?"

Will didn't have to look to know Jack was scowling. He laid his head on Jack's shoulder and burrowed under the covers to be as close to him as possible. "Yeah, even him... especially him. I couldn't face it. Felt like I had to hold on to what happened between you and me, you know? Like I was scared I'd never get that feeling back."

Jack kissed Will's head in answer, and Will knew he understood.

"I'd like to, though," Will said after a while. "With you. I think about it a lot."

Jack hummed lazily. "Me too, but you might have to wait a while. Don't think I can move."

A quiet settled over them then. Will wondered if Jack had fallen asleep, until he let out a sigh that sounded pretty bloody awake.

Will raised his head. "What's wrong?"

"Nothing. Not really, anyway. S'pose I'm just fretting about what happens now."

Will's heart sank. He'd hoped the glow of being naked in bed together would tide them over at least until morning. He groped around the bed and found Jack's hand. "I need to book a flight for tomorrow night. I've got deadlines I can't miss."

"I've got a flight to catch too," Jack said. "I've got to meet the big bosses in Berlin on Wednesday."

That got Will's attention. Jack had only been summoned to XS headquarters in Germany once to Will's knowledge, and that had been right at the start, before he'd landed the job in Ibiza. "What do they want?"

Jack bit his lip, a sure sign he was nervous. "They don't want anything. It's me doing the asking."

"What are you asking them for?"

"A new job." Jack shifted, wincing a little. "I talked to Ray today. That's where I was while you were sulking on my steps. I told him everything and asked his advice."

"What did he say?"

Jack shrugged. "Lots of things. I don't know why I didn't talk to him sooner. He thinks we might be able to figure something out. Maybe get me a residency in London and some more studio time, see if the heat, or lack of it, makes any difference. I told him I never got headaches when I played back home."

Will's heart boomed in his ears. "You're coming back to the UK?"

"Maybe. We talked about it and I want to, but it would take some negotiating to make it happen. The board has to decide I'm worth it first."

"Bollocks." Will sat up. "I've seen you play, the crowds you pull, and the way they respond to you. You're so fucking worth it, Jack. They have to know that."

Jack smiled, though it didn't quite reach his eyes. "Will, listen to me. Nothing's going to happen overnight, but I need to know this is real. You and me. I can't come home and still be a million miles from you. I can't do it anymore."

Will grabbed Jack's face and searched for his gaze until their eyes locked. "This is real, Jack. I promise."

EPILOGUE

April 2005

Leeds

JACK shut his laptop and rubbed his face as the train rumbled into the station. The journey from London, via Birmingham, had felt longer than usual. Perhaps because he'd spent all day in dull-as-rocks meetings, or maybe just because he was so eager to get to his destination.

The train stopped. Jack was first off. He jogged through the bustling station, a baseball cap pulled low over his face, and jumped in a taxi. "Headingley, please."

The driver nodded and pulled into the city's chaotic one-way system. Jack sat back and let the scenery fly by. It was Monday, the start of the working week for most people, but for him, a long weekend of DJ-ing, mixing in the studio, and meetings with mortgage advisors was finally coming to an end. He'd made the journey between Leeds and London six times in the last seven days, and he was exhausted. He needed his bed, or, more accurately, Will's bed, because whatever day of the week, there was nowhere Jack would rather be.

He paid the taxi driver and reached Will's house as Suki was dashing out of the front door. She kissed Jack's cheek in passing.

"You need to rescue your boy from his bedroom. He's been down there all day."

Jack grinned. He liked Suki. She looked out for Will, and she didn't ask them weird questions about their sex life. "I'll try. Is he in a good mood?"

Suki shrugged and went on her way, leaving Jack to face the music alone. Will had been grumpy the last few weeks, caught up in his end-of-year project, the final assessments that would determine the results of three years of hard work. Jack was more proud of him than he could say, but at the moment? Yeah. The bloke was like a bear with a sore head… a lean, blond bear, with the greenest eyes Jack had ever seen.

He trod softly downstairs to Will's basement room and dumped his bag in the corner. Will, lost in his work with his headphones on, didn't look up, and Jack took a moment to observe him unnoticed. Recently, with Will so distracted, it had become one of his favorite pastimes. Will's concentrated frown, his mussed-up hair, the tip of his tongue poking through his teeth as he polished and perfected whatever design wizardry he was working on.

Jack loved it all, drank it all in, but today he found himself captivated by the subtle arch of Will's neck. All those years they'd lived in each other's pockets, how had he not noticed how perfect it was?

"You're doing that staring thing again."

Jack jumped, startled. "Thought you had your tunes on."

"I did, though technically, they were your tunes. I was listening to that demo CD you brought home. Forgot to put something else on when it finished." Will clicked through a few screens and spun his chair round to face Jack. "You're early. Didn't think you'd make it back till midnight."

Jack grimaced, because that was a good day when he worked in London. If he was DJ-ing, he was often away for days at a time, which hadn't mattered so much while Will was caught up with uni work, but that was about to change.

Final marks depending, Will had landed a job right here in Leeds that would leave him no time to traipse around after Jack, so they needed a plan, and Jack reckoned he had one. "It's Monday, mate. I didn't have a gig today, remember?"

Will frowned. "Oh, yeah. Sorry. I keep thinking it's Friday. The weekend passed me by. Where've you been today? You were in Bristol last night, right? Or was that last week?"

Jack rolled his eyes. "That was three weeks ago. I was in Brixton last night, and Kensington this morning."

That got Will's attention. The only reason for Jack to be in Kensington was to meet with his management team at his record company's UK headquarters. "What were you doing there? Everything okay?"

Jack resisted the urge to yank Will from his chair and into his arms. "More than okay. You know how I've been doing more work in the production studio?"

Will nodded. Away from the oppressive heat and relentless schedule of Ibiza, Jack's migraines were under control, but Jack had found a renewed passion in production work that had faded while he'd been distracted by a packed itinerary of live shows. "Is this about them shutting down the studios in Brick Lane? Does this mean you have to go abroad again?"

"Nope." Jack shook his head, gleeful. This had been in the pipeline for a few months, but he hadn't told Will in case it fell through. "They're not shutting them down. They're relocating them... to Nottingham."

"Nottingham? You mean... you'll be able to work up here sometimes?"

Jack's grin widened. "It's better than that, mate. They want me to produce and coordinate their next six albums, as well as my own, which means—"

"Fuck! You can live up here?"

Jack laughed. "Yeah, I mean, if you want me to? I'll still have to play gigs in London sometimes, and in the summer, they reckon they might send me to LA for a few weeks, but you could come with me. You get holidays, right? And I want to play more free parties, and join a band again, and—"

Will tackled Jack to the bed, cutting him off with a crazed kiss. Jack let him have his way a moment. He'd been gone all weekend, and he'd missed this... missed Will. He often felt like he had a limb missing when they weren't together.

He lost himself in Will for a while. He'd fought the heat between them for so long, these days it felt like they could spend all day wrapped up in each other and he'd still go to sleep craving more.

Will kissed the hell out of him, ripped his T-shirt off, and fumbled with his belt. Jack gave him a hand and made short work of the tracksuit bottoms he suspected Will had, between showers, been wearing all weekend.

Naked, they wrestled and rolled their way to the middle of the bed. Despite his leaner frame, Will ended up on top, which was just how Jack liked it. Loved it, in fact. There was nothing better than letting Will own him, inside and out. He'd never figured himself a bottom, even during those dark days he'd spent so much time agonizing over the unwavering desire he'd harbored for Will from the moment they'd first kissed all those years ago. But a bottom he was, and as Will moved down his body with his teeth and tongue, he parted his legs and raised them, coaxing Will in... craving his touch where he needed it most.

It was all too easy to get carried away. Will worked his magic with slick fingers, and Jack arched up into him, grinding himself down on Will's cock. Will bagged up and aligned them, his gaze fixed on Jack, watching for any sign of the discomfort that had faded months ago. He pressed in. Jack gasped and bit down on Will's shoulder. This part didn't hurt anymore, but the sensation of Will filling him was as toe-curling as it had ever been.

Will was buried to the hilt and building up a wicked rhythm before Jack remembered he had more to tell him. If this was a fuck to celebrate their future, there was something else Will needed to know.

"Oh, God. Fuck, wait. I need to tell you something."

Will raised his head from his devilish assault on Jack's neck. "Not leaving me for a bird, are you?"

"What? Fuck, no." Jack gripped Will hard enough to leave bruises on his pale skin. With Will easing his cock in and out of Jack, clouding his mind with a sweet push and slide that made Jack's eyes roll, Jack was almost past the point of coherent speech, but his sexuality was an ongoing fascination for both of them. Jack was crazy about Will, but he still had little idea if Will's anatomy had anything to do with it. He'd never truly wanted another bloke. Did that make him bisexual? Jack had no idea, and he wasn't sure he cared. He loved *Will*. Nothing else mattered. "It's not about that. It's about money."

Will slowed his rhythm and fixed Jack with his best "don't fuck with me" glare. "What about it?"

"I, er, don't have any…. Least, I won't by this time next week."

"Eh?" Will stilled and rose up on his hands, his dick pulsing inside Jack, like it could go off at any moment. "Thought you had a pot of gold stashed away."

"Very funny." It was Jack's turn to glare. Will had never resented Jack's success, but he'd never cared for the idea of living off Jack's money. Good job, really. "I kinda bought a house today. My dad tried to sell my mum's house from under her. The law says he can't till Laurie leaves school, but that's not so far away so… I, uh, bought it."

"You bought your mum a house?"

"I bought *her* house for her." Jack knew Will would understand the difference. His whole family was still struggling with a year that had turned their world upside down—divorce, gay pictures in magazines. Jack hated his dad—in some ways, he always had—but his mum deserved better than to lose the home she'd tended for twenty-five years.

"So you're skint, then?" Will brought Jack back to the present with a playful tug on Jack's dick.

"Yeah, shit. *Will*." Jack gritted his teeth and tried to get a grip on himself. "I mean, I won't be for long, but I cleared all my savings to put the deposit down, and I'll have to pay the mortgage on top of wherever else we live. For a while, it's just me, my decks, and my drum kit."

Will smiled and closed his eyes. He picked up the pace of his thrusts again, adding a twist that took Jack's breath away. "I've missed that drum kit, but, Jack, I don't give a fuck how much money you have. I live in a basement and eat Pot Noodle for breakfast. As long as you're with me, I'm happy with that."

Jack had spent a long morning at the bank, and he figured they could do a little better than that, but the time for talk was over. He lay back and let Will have his way, watching through heavy eyes as Will turned them both inside out. Will was so strong, so sure of his own mind. Not like Jack, who wrestled with even the smallest things before he was sure of his path. Sometimes, only this… only Will, made sense to him.

Jack came with a low cry, spilling over his belly and Will's hand. He saw stars for a moment, like he always did when Will pushed him over the edge, but his vision cleared in time to see Will's jaw fall slack, to hear his gravelly moan and feel him lock up and release.

Will collapsed on Jack's chest, breathing hard. Jack held him close and nuzzled his tousled hair, stroking his sweat-sheened skin. He loved these moments of completion, broken only by the need to clean up and chuck the condom. Lucky for him, Will liked to do all that… liked to take care of Jack after he'd played him so hard.

Will got up. Jack remained sprawled out and dazed until Will came back, wiped them both clean, and rubbed a soothing hand over Jack's bare skin. "All right, mate?"

Jack hummed, lazy and sated. "Yeah."

"Sleepyhead." Will mussed Jack's hair.

Jack fought him off and mock scowled. "Can I ask you something?"

"Course you can." Will grabbed a pillow. He jammed it under Jack's head and rubbed Jack's temple with his thumb, the way he did when Jack had a headache.

"Remember that letter you gave to my dad?"

"Er, yeah...." Will's expression darkened slightly. He had no love for Jack's father.

"What did it say?"

"What did it say?" Will cringed. "Oh, God. I don't know. I was pretty upset when I wrote it, and nervous too. I was terrified of moving to Leeds without you. I felt really alone, you know?"

Jack's heart ached, but he understood. He'd got on a plane to Ibiza honestly believing Will didn't give a shit about what had passed between them. That he didn't even feel it.

Will sighed and tangled his fingers in Jack's hair. "I think I rambled on about being friends for life... blood brothers and all that shit. I think I even told you I loved you."

"Yeah?" Jack retrieved Will's hand and twined their fingers together. "And do you? Love me?"

Will looked down. "Course I do, you daft wanker. How could you not know that?"

Jack shrugged, because he did know it, he just needed to hear it from time to time. "I feel the same, if it's any consolation."

"You'll never be my consolation prize, Jack. You're everything I've ever wanted." Will punctuated the sweetest thing he'd ever said with a biting kiss, and then he pulled away with a grin. "I do need to get the fuck out of this room, though. How about we get dressed and I buy you a pint?"

It was the best offer Jack had heard all day. A pint with his best mate? Life didn't get much better that that. "You're on, and Will?"

"Yeah?"

"I love you too."

108

NEWSLETTER

Get a free story!

For the most up to date news and free books, subscribe to my newsletter HERE.

This is a zero spam zone. Maximum number of emails you will receive is one per month.

PATREON

Not ready to let go of Will and Jack? Or looking for sneak peeks at future books in the series? Alternative POVs, outtakes, and missing moments from **all** Garrett's books can be found on her Patreon site. Misfits, Slide, Strays...the works. Because you know what? Garrett wasn't ready to let her boys go either.

Pledges start from as little as $2, and all content is available at the lowest tier.

FURTHER READING

Missing Will and Jack already? You can get a glimpse of their attempts at adult life in Lucky Man.

ABOUT GARRETT LEIGH

Bonus Material available for all books on Garrett's Patreon account. Includes short stories from Misfits, Slide, Strays, What Remains, Dream, and much more. Sign up here: https://www.patreon.com/garrettleigh

Facebook Fan Group, Garrett's Den... https://www.facebook.com/groups/garre...

Garrett Leigh is an award-winning British writer, cover artist, and book designer. Her debut novel, Slide, won Best Bisexual Debut at the 2014 Rainbow Book Awards, and her polyamorous novel, Misfits was a finalist in the 2016 LAMBDA awards, and was again a finalist in 2017 with Rented Heart.

In 2017, she won the EPIC award in contemporary romance with her military novel, Between Ghosts, and the contemporary romance category in the Bisexual Book Awards with her novel What Remains.

When not writing, Garrett can generally be found procrastinating on Twitter, cooking up a storm, or sitting on her behind doing as little as possible, all the while shouting at her menagerie of children and animals and attempting to tame her unruly and wonderful FOX.

Garrett is also an award winning cover artist, taking the silver medal at the Benjamin Franklin Book Awards in 2016. She designs for various publishing houses and independent authors at blackjazzdesign.com, and co-owns the specialist stock site moonstockphotography.com

Connect with Garrett
www.garrettleigh.com

ALSO BY GARRETT LEIGH

Lucky Man

Finding Home

Only Love

Heart

What Remains

What Matters

Between Ghosts

Printed in Great Britain
by Amazon